BRIAN CASTRO
BIRDS OF PASSAGE

*un*tapped

ABOUT *UNTAPPED*

Most Australian books ever written have fallen out of print and become unavailable for purchase or loan from libraries. This includes important local and national histories, biographies and memoirs, beloved children's titles, and even winners of glittering literary prizes such as the Miles Franklin Literary Award.

Supported by funding from state and territory libraries, philanthropists and the Australian Research Council, *Untapped* is identifying Australia's culturally important lost books, digitising them, and promoting them to new generations of readers. As well as providing access to lost books and a new source of revenue for their writers, the *Untapped* collaboration is supporting new research into the economic value of authors' reversion rights and book promotion by libraries, and the relationship between library lending and digital book sales. The results will feed into public policy discussions about how we can better support Australian authors, readers and culture.

See untapped.org.au for more information, including a full list of project partners and rediscovered books.

Readers are reminded that these books are products of their time. Some may contain language or reflect views that might now be found offensive or inappropriate.

For Jo

CONTENTS

CONTENTS

O the mind, mind has mountains; cliffs of fall
Frightful, sheer, no-man-fathomed. Hold them
cheap
May who ne'er hung there.

Gerard Manley Hopkins

If there had been no Chinese here, Australians
might have almost invented them. Every society at
times needs its scapegoat, its target; and it was almost as if the Chinese were the yardstick by which
the British in Australia judged themselves, and
they judged themselves to be pretty good. They
complained that the Chinese were insanitary and
that on the diggings they polluted the water. They
complained that the Chinese were birds of passage
who were eager to leave Australia, taking away
the gold at the earliest possible moment. They
complained that the Chinese were heathen. They
were addicted to drugs—opium rather than alcohol—and were the supreme gamblers. Curiously,
a version of all these complaints could have been
directed against many of the British diggers on the
goldfields. The Chinese were specially vulnerable
because they were different, and were easily identi-
fied. Moreover, they were here in disturbingly large
numbers. In 1859 one in every nine men in Australia was Chinese.

Geoffrey Blainey, *The Blainey View*

1 THE OTHER LIFE

Kwangtung, 1856

My name is Lo Yun Shan. I take my name from Tai Mo Shan, which is the Big Mist Mountain. The mountain is not very high by Chinese standards, but it is constantly shrouded in cloud and mist. No one has ever viewed the summit from afar, even on the brightest days. The village people say that the Buddha lives on the summit, and from there he maintains his indifferent gaze on the valleys below. If you climb the mountain from the east, you will see a small temple jutting out of the rock. In the interior of the temple you will see a huge Buddha carved out of stone. No one is permitted to climb higher than the temple. To do so would be disrespectful and, worse, would bring bad luck.

I have taken the climb above the temple; I have reached the summit and felt the moisture of the clouds. Time and time again I have gone to the summit in my youth. There I found peace. I also found evidence of other climbers ... half-eaten bags of rice and vegetables, wrapped in banana leaves; fish bones; human faeces congealed in the cold.

I was a young teacher then. I had a certain iconoclastic view of life. To be a teacher in those times meant that you had a spiritual connection with the heavens. Your word was law among the ignorant. Given your knowledge, your power, you were almost expected to flout some of the rules governing the less enlightened. I was somewhere between a monk and an administrator. I sat on the village executive, I presided over minor judicial matters as my father's proxy. I had been trained by the monks in the temple, and my family was one of the best in the province.

My father wore a long gown and received taxes from the villagers. I was his principal tax-collector, walking from farm to farm among the different hamlets of our region when the weather was fine. When it was wet I sat snug in my rocking sedan chair and listened to the squelching steps of the coolies, the box emitting a not unpleasant perfumed mustiness in contrast to the humid air outside, the harsh wetness glistening on the long poles and bare, heaving torsos, redolent of sweat. Behind was the barrow, filled with bags of rice, squealing pigs and flapping ducks.

My father sat in his house with his opium pipe. Before entering, I would smell the sweetness of the smoke from his room, and when there was a breeze in the summer I would hear the bells tinkle over the door and see the long pieces of prayer-paper tied to them fluttering in the wind.

My father, dressed in his long embroidered gown, would motion me in with his free hand. Sometimes he would stop me from speaking by presenting his palm in a salute and taking his pipe from his mouth with a sucking sound and a deep intake of breath. The pipe would sizzle and hiss. Then he would say:

'Listen to the petals. The petals of the jasmine flower are falling.'

I accepted his eccentricities. I had no time for poetry or such musings; and in this I shared the characteristics of the Kwangtung people. We are businesslike; we want to get on in the world. We live for barter, trade, catties of rice—the essentials of society and communality. A poet like my father sets himself apart. It is a privilege. Starving peasants rarely become poets.

Allowing my father his half-minute of silence, I would then make my report: 20 catties of rice per holding (20 kans or approximately 27 lb.), 6 ducklings, 2 suckling pigs.

My father would nod, smile, and I would go out and deal with other business.

Every two months I used to make the short trip to the coast.

I looked forward to this trip with boundless enthusiasm. I loved the sea, the bare hills dotted with boulders leading down to the sea, the windswept headland, the salt stinging my cheeks. These sensations I kept hidden within myself. They were my treasures, metaphoric vaults containing curiosity and excitement. But I realize now how the sea, which taught me so much about life, ultimately strangled my curiosity and led me to meaninglessness; led me to believe that human beings, intent on viewing the ultimate, see only as far as themselves.

Sydney
NAME: O'YOUNG, SEAMUS
Nom
Place and Date of Birth
Lieu et Date de Naissance
Height
Taille
Colour of Eyes
Couleur des Yeux
Colour of Hair
Couleur des Cheveux
Visible Peculiarities
Signes Particuliers

My passport lies open on the table. Its empty pages marked with the word VISAS tease my imagination. My stub of a pencil trembles over them for it is here that I will begin my journey.

Beside me I have the fragments of a journal. I found them a long time ago, stuck to my memory like the remnants of a dream. I have read and re-read those words, translated and re-translated them, deciphering the strokes of the Chinese characters, building up their meaning, constructing and reconstructing their sense. I feel the closeness of the situation the author is describing; I feel I am the counterpart of this man who was writing more than a century ago. The similarity of his situation to mine does not disturb me as much as the almost complete identification of his style, choice of words and tonality with my own. The only difference is his calm, in contrast to my frenzy and apprehension; a deceitful calm perhaps, in the discipline of those serene brush strokes. Perhaps the intervening years of decaying language and translation are to blame.

But why do I feel such an anxiety about the influence of his style, such a sense of guilt as I carry his writing around with me, the yellow pages already worn to the thinness of butterfly wings? (I have taken the precaution of enfolding them in contact plastic.) It is possible that these shards of the past have invested me with a responsibility for another life, demanding that I write honestly. But how can I when my mind is already dislocated by so many illusions, illusions that have sprung from my self-imposed solitude? At times haunted by this *Doppelgänger*, I have tried to exorcize it, imagining flames consuming the fragile written record, history coiled in those wisps of smoke climbing heavenward; but again the yellow pages have resisted obliteration. So now I carry them with me as talismans for other points of departure.

I hear the voices of children rattling the panes as another afternoon comes to its end. The shadows of leaves and patches of light dart about behind the curtains. A strong wind is blowing. I hope it will not rain. There is a strangeness about the coolness: the leaves, the night ready to open up its secret grottoes, all the fragrances of solemnity. In the sadness of this early evening I am aware of the shapes of dreams departing.

I recall now, at this stage of my journal, one of the first trips to the coast I made in that drought-stricken year. Until that trip my mind had been enclosed by the village; it wandered around like a trapped tiger. Sometimes when I came home in the evenings I would see the shadow of my mother in a dark corner of the house. She would be sitting, having entered the solitude of her illness, waiting for her thoughts to regroup, to send them out again, testing the borders. My mind roared with anguish at the way her world had closed upon her.

I will never forget the first time I viewed the sea. I saw its soft green stretching like fields to the horizon. Never before had my eyes been tested by such distance. I believed that I had found the gateway to the world. Then I saw the port below me like something the sea had vomited up, rejected, cast upon the beach. The town was piled upon itself in a hotch-potch of shacks, shanties, two-storeyed wooden buildings in disrepair. Narrow alleyways and streets ran in no rational manner, some turning around upon themselves, like the people, who walked with heads turned backwards; poverty-stricken, belligerent, mistrustful. Children defecated in the streets. Old men, finding the squat beyond their years, and without a thought for modesty, urinated, thin, yellow streams pulsing from their cupped hands.

With each visit to the port I noticed a worsening despair on the faces of the people. They looked away from me when formerly they used to stare at strangers. Heads down, they hunched into their own preoccupations.

One wet day, while studying them from my box, a beggar came up to me and attached his grimy fingers to my sleeve, hobbling alongside, focusing the liquid whiteness of his bad eye on my face. I pulled my hand away, and ordered the chair coolies to increase their speed. The beggar kept pace, his shaven head bobbing beside me. I leant back into my box and reached for a coin, but then I hesitated, my warring conscience having reached a stalemate. The shaven head disappeared in a stream of curses.

Avoiding the puddles in the wet street, outpacing the cursing beggar and trying to keep away from the damp walls, my coolies set me down before the wooden shack which was the goal of my journey. It stood before the reddish stone wall at one extremity

of the town. Above the door, written in red letters was the name
of my father's business partner. It said:

Ship Chandlery
So Ah Fung — Proprietor

In the dark shop my eye caught a movement, a glistening
of flesh in the corner. A figure approached me from among
huge coils of rope. Gradually my eyes grew accustomed to
the darkness, and I made out a woman holding a baby to her
breast. Her dark hair was plaited in huge hempen pigtails and
in between these two snakes was coiled her baby, asleep at the
drooping breast, the nipple fiery and glowing. It was Ah Fung's
wife. She nodded to me, her smile radiating into a crescent,
revealing a row of golden teeth.

'Ah, Shan. You've come at a bad time.'

I didn't know what she meant.

'Perhaps I'll return later.'

No, she didn't mean the baby. She pointed her chin towards
the door.

'There's trouble in town. Foreign soldiers.'

The baby squirmed, began to cry. Outside the coolies were
playing checkers, squatting on the ground, shouting, slapping
each other on the back.

'How is your mother?'

'Still the same.'

'Your father?'

'He's well. He sends his greetings.'

I resolved to stay no longer than necessary, my eyes trans-
fixed by her pale breast, its nipple like the sunset. She went behind the counter, brought out two cloth bags, and opened them
for me with her free hand. I took out some of the opium and
sniffed at it.

'This will have to be the last,' she said, 'They are thinking of
closing the port, of stamping out the smuggling.'

'Aiyeeee!' the coolies were yelling. The game had become serious. They spat into their hands, cursing and muttering. The baby screamed. Ah Fung's wife rocked it back and forth. She smiled at me and I gave her the bag of coins. She didn't count them, so I bade her farewell and left the shop.

My task completed, I took the bags, placed them under the seat in the box and told the chair coolies to wait for me. I then allowed my mind to take in all the aspects of the town.

I noticed particularly the presence of our soldiers, clad in their ancient armour, patrolling sections of the town. In one alleyway I saw an old man drop his baskets and the long bamboo pole attached to them and run quickly away in an absurd, bow-legged canter. At the other end of the alley two soldiers appeared, cutting off his retreat. He was seized immediately, and fell to the ground under blows from heavy clubs. I did not stop to look any longer. On the waterfront groups of pale-faced foreign sailors paced nervously up and down. Several Chinese officials, dressed in their long gowns and balancing comically in a bobbing sampan, were heading out towards the mouth of the river.

I am back at the edge of the sea; with the wind, with the water; my eyes burning, my mind confused; my knowledge suddenly exposed as a vast ignorance.

A tall ship appears in the drizzle under two small sails. Huge as a temple, like a whale surfacing among the sardine-shaped fishing-boats, it symbolizes the powerful ingress of a foreign race. I suspect immediately that their industry is a hundred times vaster and more precise than ours, that their penetration of China this time will be deeper and more violent.

The ship drops its anchor and swings into the wind. The officials on the sampan are approaching it with speed, the oarsman leaning with all his strength on the pole. A fluttering banner of red, white and blue is run up on the ship's ratlines as the officials clamber on to the gangway.

I didn't stay to watch the proceedings, to witness the Chinese officials lowering the Union Jack, to share that moment in history leading to the second war with the foreigners. On my way home, in my swaying sedan chair, it was difficult to imagine that what I had under the seat was the cause of so much trouble in China. I thought of our feuding clans, my somnolent father, the beating the old man had received. I felt my loyalties divide. On an impulse, I spat in the direction of the temple on the hill overlooking the town.

Seamus O'Young. It's not my real name. I'm not Irish. I am in fact an ABC; that is, an Australian-born Chinese. Yes and no. I find your questions infuriating. People are always very curious about nationality. They will go to great lengths to pigeonhole someone. They think this knowledge gives them *power*.

I remember entering the UK at Folkstone on the car-ferry. The customs officer looked at me for a long time while holding my passport. In the next queue a black girl was shouting and screaming.

'You are bloody-minded,' she shrieked.

The customs man turned towards the shouting. Then he said to me, 'So you're one of these bloody Chinese-born Australians.'

Before I was able to correct him, he waved me through with his head turned. Behind, the shouting intensified.

Yes. ABC. The first three letters of the alphabet. It was a classification which straddled two cultures. Yes. ABC. I am a refugee, an exile. My heart and my head are in the wrong places. There was no country from which I came, and there is none to which I can return. I do not speak Chinese, but I am learning it. At the institute where I attend classes they think I am a little strange.

I believe my real name is Sham Oh Yung, but I am unable to find any records of my past. I am a truly stateless person. When I go to Chinatown I feel at one with the people, but then the strange tones of their language only serve to isolate me.

I was an orphan, and I like to believe that I was tough,

hard-boiled, as they say, when I was a kid. I never worried about being classified. I was in a special school because they thought I was mentally handicapped: on account of my appearance they had labelled me as 'Mongoloid'. When I grew older they realized their mistake, and I was transferred to a normal school. It was then that I was adopted by the Groves. It was also then that I began to think about my appearance. The pupils at the normal school called me names. At first I enjoyed it, as a clown enjoys entertaining others, sublimating the irony of laughing at himself. Then I began to invent fictions of my past.

I dreamt (usually in class) that my father was a visiting seaman (the pun unnoticed at the time) from Manchuria; that he was a descendant of a great Manchurian lord. I dreamt that he stepped ashore in Sydney, off his oceangoing junk which was furnished in the fashion of elaborate Chinese temples; that he was entertained by all the society ladies of the North Shore; and that he fell in love with one of them, a rich heiress with blue eyes. I dreamt that her parents forbade their marriage, and so they eloped and went to live in a grand house in Point Piper. While my mother was pregnant, lying in her feather bed, the descendant of the Manchurian lord weighed anchor and slipped out of Sydney. In despair and shame, my mother placed me in an orphanage.

It was always at this stage in my dream, with an idiotic smile on my face, that Brother Pius would crack me hard over the head with a ruler for daydreaming. Brother Pius, the Inquisitor, who could give six of the best and open boys' tender hands to the realities of life, for masturbation or just plain fiddling; Brother Pius, history teacher and choirmaster, continually plagued with the voices of boys whose hormones refused to be regulated; Brother Pius, part-time librarian, who handed out books by G.K. Chesterton, G.K. Chesterton and G.K. Chesterton, whose Irish breath smelt of whisky and who leant over me with the ruler under my nose.

'What year was gold discovered in Australia?' He tapped at

my cheek with the ruler. I did not know the answer.

'O'Young. What kind of a name is that?' he asked.

You see, I have blue eyes. That is why I could not be completely Chinese. I used to think long and hard about this when
I was a schoolboy. Every morning I used to look into the mirror
at my blue eyes, and I used to think of where they could have
come from. One day I asked my best friend in the playground to
describe me. This is how he saw me:

'You have a moonface,' he said, 'with black hair sticking out
of the top and your eyes are slits. Your nose is flat and you have
yellow skin.'

Upon my return to the village, my mother was in the third
month of her long period of illness. She lay on the low bed in
her room, her drawn face exhibiting the burdens of her life and
the beginnings of her preoccupation with death.

My mother has been a shadow these last few years. She has
kept apart from my father and myself. She lived, as a woman
does, with the worries and anxieties that are incomprehensible
in the world of men. Men live with the pragmatism of the self.
For a man, his mind totally closed off by his self, it is difficult to
understand that a woman can chafe over the terrible responsibility of love. I have heard my mother moan in the night. Hers is
a silent moan which pierces the firmament.

Yet I was glad to return. At least in the village there is order,
growing out of the necessity to live within a social framework
that respects the seasons, work, and the sanctity of life. I was
glad that I did not live in the town among the fishermen whose
harvest from the sea seemed to me a harvest of violence, of
thievery, of piracy; for they do nothing for the sea. They are
not in harmony with it, because they do not raise the fish. The
abundant sea is for plundering, destroying. Perhaps this is why
the boat people and the village people have never intermarried.

My mother's brother, Ah Fung, has been an anomaly. He
went from being a farmer to a storekeeper at the port. Because

he married a woman from the town, the relationship between him and our family was severed. My father, however, continued to do business through Ah Fung's wife. Since his marriage, I had never seen my uncle, though I was curious about his shadowy reputation. He was said to be a member of several secret societies.

When my father insisted on my buying more bags of opium, Ah Fung's wife relented and said that she would do what she could. She took my father's money and said she would have the opium on my next trip. When I arrived at the ship chandlery two months later Ah Fung's wife told me that he had signed the store over to her and he had gone off on a foreign vessel. She did not seem to know where he had gone. There was no opium and Ah Fung had taken all the money.

My return from the port that final time filled me with sadness. Upon reaching the house, I saw the banners of white cloth at the door. On them, the black characters announced the solemnity of a death within. I knew it was my mother. She had finally attained peace. I cannot remember exactly how I felt at the time. I followed, I think, the usual emotional channels within myself, seeking the meaning of their source. On the outside, I behaved according to the proprieties accepted by my people. Weeping was out of the question. A stoic resolution pervaded my senses, but every now and again I felt a gush of emotion I was unable to control. In retrospect I do not think it was sadness. It was a sort of claustrophobia, of wanting to be somewhere else; or, more precisely, of wanting to be everywhere at once. It was an aching, breathless feeling, making me totally incapable of action. The smells, sights, sounds, coming from within the house limited and frustrated me; and yet they were the only means, the only windows as it were, through which I could escape.

Even before I entered the passageway to my mother's room I could hear the clanging bells and gongs of the monks. I was angry at these paid mourners, these vicarious purveyors of emotion and pathos. At the end of their solemn and bizarre

performance by the side of the corpse, my father would hand
out little red envelopes of money, envelopes printed with prayers
in gold letters that would flutter up to the heavens; and then
my mother would begin to be the object of our own worship
and reverence. We would bring offerings of food to her grave
periodically; food for the dead to keep the spirit alive. Then we
would have a banquet there on the hillside, while the urchins
waited patiently eyeing the food and, upon our departure,
would leap on to the grave to devour what was left.

When I reached her room I could smell the strong scent of
the incense. The chanting and the gongs were deafening. The
room was filled with smoke. Seven monks lined the way to my
mother's bed, their shaven heads glistening with sweat, their
robes coming undone in their frenzy. When they saw me they
intensified their mourning. I reached my mother's bedside. Her
face had not changed dramatically from the time I left her; perhaps now there was more of an artificiality about it. Her grief
was a sculptured one, and now her expression was fixed for
ever, open to the interpretations of the viewers in the gallery.

Mother. My mother. The monks whipped themselves into
louder appeals, their voices rising in pitch. The smoke brought
tears to my eyes, and through it, across the bobbing heads, my
father emerged, as though walking on a cloud, in his black and
silver embroidered gown, his feet encased in silken slippers, his
eyes painted, his fingernails an inch long. There was a solemn
expression on his face beneath the cake of white paint, and his
red lips were pursed tight over the wispy beard. He held a fan
to his chest, and as he walked he fanned away the smoke with
dainty movements. He bowed and kissed the shining dome of
the nearest monk, then he proceeded towards my mother, his
face inscrutable and scandalous at the same time, licensed by
the unspoken acceptance in our society of the transvestism of
those who are spiritual. I left the room in horror.

'Welcome to the family,' Jack Grove said, extending a huge hand the size of a shovel. He then handed me a whisky. I was twelve years old at the time.

I had come from a boys' home to the Groves's Sydney suburban cottage. It was a dark brick house with an iron roof that sloped down on to the oleanders near the front fence. By the front door there was a brass plate that said NIRVANA. I was curious about what that meant. I thought it was the capital of Cuba. There was a lot about Cuba on the news.

Inside the house it was always dark. There were two front bedrooms, Jack occupying one and his wife the other. I had the back room with its pastel-coloured walls and blue linoleum floor. In the living-room Jack's rack of shotguns shared the wall with his wife's glass-fronted bookcases. Porcelain ducks flew across the gunsights.

Jack and Edna Grove were well-meaning but incompetent foster parents. Jack worked at a shoe factory, making orthopaedic shoes. He hammered heels into shoes made for clubbed feet with his fists, fashioned and worked the leather with his fingers, pulled out nails with his teeth which had convenient gaps in the front. He got up at five in the morning, was at work by six, and by eleven he would have drunk almost half a bottle of whisky, which he kept on the shelf behind his bench. By one in the afternoon he would be into his second bottle. It was fortunate for him that his boss drank along with him. It was also fortunate that Jack finished work at two in the afternoon. He would stagger on to the 438 bus and arrive home silent, withdrawn, incomprehensible.

Edna, meanwhile, had gone about the housework with enthusiasm. She too had taken frequent nips out of the brandy bottle she kept in the cistern in the toilet. By three in the afternoon she had a rosy, smiling face. She was quite happy as a drunk.

When I got home from school at four they would both be asleep, loud snores coming from their room. I would then begin to make myself some dinner, for Jack and Edna rarely ate. During my first few months with them, Edna used to prepare rice dishes for me. She left the rice simmering on the stove for hours before I got home, and I would often find a hard, blackened cake of rice at the bottom of the saucepan. Edna would be asleep. She was surprised when I told her one night that I didn't like rice dishes, and that I liked pies, steaks and chips.

I suppose that it was about this time that I took to making my own meals and began to take a big interest in food. I cannot forget the great joy I took in eating, the expertise with which I prepared my meals. These were the happiest days of my life. But then my life with them changed.

Something was happening. Jack came home earlier and earlier. I stopped going to school; Edna and Jack sat for hours at the kitchen table staring at the table-cloth or the walls. One day Jack did not go to work. He locked himself in the garage and got drunk early. Edna went to the toilet and stayed there for hours. There was no lock on the toilet door. Every time I approached it I would hear her clear her throat, to let me know she was in there. I could also hear the brandy bottle being placed on the tiled floor.

On the day Jack's father died of cirrhosis of the liver I ate four sausage rolls and two pies without thinking how that death would affect my life. Two weeks later we moved to the country, to the property left to Jack which was called *Twin Groves*, and was famous for its unproductive soil. I sat in the back of the truck with the furniture and watched puffs of rain and exhaust fumes recede into the landscape. Edna's books curled their wings and tried to fly out of their boxes.

We moved into a corrugated-iron farmhouse that was exposed to the bitterness of winter and the seething irritation of summer. Everywhere I uncovered signs of an old man: half-chewed pipe stems, carved walking-sticks, broken spectacles. In the machinery shed I found countless dark-green and brown bottles stacked neatly from floor to roof, dark catacombs for the secret lives of spiders. I began my new life in a fug of depression, hypnotized myself out of it with backbreaking work, and even believed I loved the chalky sterility of the land. I became lean, strong, and I grew hungrier.

Machinery began to break down, with no hope of its being repaired. Jack spent less and less time maintaining the old tractor. Everything fell to pieces, or was tied with wire: makeshift ways for a makeshift existence. Edna and Jack drank openly now that the world was falling down and propriety was no virtue.

I remember that I was coming in from the fields, swearing and cursing at the piece of metal I held in my hand, watching the light fade in the west, dreading the hours I would have to spend in the dark fumbling with cut knuckles and raw fingers in the greasy maw of the engine. The tin shed smelt of dog droppings and kerosene. As I approached the bench I noticed a figure sitting on a box in the corner. The half-light quickened my senses. I expected an intruder; Jack's twin brother returned from the Melbourne docks, wanting his share of the land; Bill Grove, also known as Fitzpatrick, or 'Clancy', with a past as shadowy as the pine forest bordering the house. But the dogs were there, lying in the dust, their tails dabbing at the ground like tiny movements of a feather-duster.

I approached the figure, saw that it was watching me from under the hat. I lit a match. It was Jack; it could not have been his twin. The face was gloomy, there was the usual bottle next to him; he was paralytic.

I swore at him and tried to lift him, feeling the cold skin of his arm around my neck. There was no foul breath hot against the side of my face. I propped him back on the box and he seemed to groan; but his face was waxen and his eyes stared glassily at his feet under half-closed lids. A crow cawed its way between the hills. Jack Grove was dead. I stood guard over him, flicking away the spiders emerging from their glass mountain, lighting match after match for the passage of his soul.

In that quiet hour I let Edna sleep, floating in her alcoholic vapours. I sat down beside Jack and talked to him, asked him the hundred or so questions to which he had failed to provide the answers. I wanted this experience of death to be mine alone. Jack had all the answers now.

When I lit the kerosene lamp I noticed the empty bottle of brake fluid on the bench next to the box on which Jack was sitting, having his last drink, putting an indelible full-stop to his life. I went back to fix the tractor, and then drove in to get Doctor Williams.

Edna refused to accept Jack's death. She spoke to him in the bathroom, called out to him from the kitchen. She began to talk in long rambling sentences. Doc Williams took her away to the clinic in town. When I visited her she was painting still lifes, oil on canvas.

'They say it's therapeutic,' she said. She wanted her books.

I glanced at her paintings. Each one was of a full bottle of Napoleon brandy.

Two weeks later I left Twin Groves and went back to the boys' home in the city. It was my first experience of running away.

The experiences we have in childhood, including those in our dreams, bring us closer to death than those of our adult years. I remember when I was about six watching the death of my little sister in the river that runs beside our village. I watched her swim towards me from the bank, past where she could just stand on tiptoe on the muddy bottom, and then I saw her small body caught by the current which swept her away. During her struggle I saw a look of peace rather than panic on her face as she went under. I dreamt about her death year after year, until I was part of it, falling back into unconsciousness from the dream. In it I experienced what it was like not to exist, a transition from one consciousness to another. In my dream I was my sister, and then at the point of her death I became myself. In the intervening moment during the transition I experienced death.

My mother's death did not have the same effect on me as my sister's death.

Jack had taught me how to skin foxes. On cold cloudy mornings, when the wind is crisp and the dust is blown off the sides of hills, foxes will trot up to a whistle, cocking their heads and presenting their white chests to the terrible force of bullets.

When the steam puffs out of the hole with each gushing of blood, you take a very small sharp knife, cut along the inside of each hind-leg, peeling back the skin to the belly. You do the same with the fore-legs, lopping away some of the fat sticking to the flesh. Then you go up the middle, peeling the skin from the throat and back, chop lightly around the base of the ears, circumcising the nose. You then tie the skin from a hind-leg around the base of the tail, pull hard, your foot on the head, and the tail emerges from its skin like the inside of a sausage. Finally you draw the skin over the head and you hold in your hand a still warm fur, the blood now drying on your trousers to a dark brown rust. Behind you the carcass looks like a new-born rat with fur booties.

Back in the city, living at the boys' home, I wandered through the wet streets along the harbourside thinking of foxes. One morning, from a dark doorway, a man emerged holding a large kitchen knife, running towards me.

'You bastard,' he screamed at me, his fly undone, his face twisted in extreme anger.

I ran like a fox, and did not understand his anger.

My father could buy no more opium. Everywhere the fields dried up and the farmers were unable to pay taxes. Soldiers thundered through the village on horseback, leaving clouds of dust to settle on my father's perplexed face. Groups of young men looted houses. My students, civilized boys learning to read and write, suddenly became hard-faced youths speaking fierce-ly of anarchy and war.

Fook, my prize-pupil, the one who was making the most progress in writing and who was even beginning to write a few lines of poetry, called on me one day. He had on a long grey gown, his big cane hat, and he carried a folding stick of cloth he had purchased at the port from a tall foreign 'devil'. He showed it off to me, opening and closing it, asking me to feel its lightness, trying to convince me that it had a practical purpose instead of a purely decorative one.

Screwing up his pimply face so that he looked like a ten-year-old instead of the eighteen-year-old he really was, he began to talk to me in an offensive manner.

'Lessons are over now,' he said. 'We don't want your lessons any more. Most of the boys have gone away to the port with their fathers.'

'What are you talking about?' I asked, and then in a firmer tone I said, 'And to whom do you think you are speaking?'

He backed off a little from the doorstep and looked at me half timidly, half aggressively.

'There is a lot of talk about gold in a land to the south. Some people have already returned from there with bags of it. So what d'you say to that, eh? What d'you say? Are you going? Like the rest of us? I'll make a fortune, you'll see. I won't give a hang about the weather, about this stinking life.'

Then he did a dance, turning round and round the stick of cloth he held in his left hand. I didn't know what to make of him as he then trailed it behind him and smiled at me while he walked down the road, his big hat catching the low branches of the trees.

I went back inside, my head filled with a thousand ideas. Of course I had heard the talk to which Fook referred. It was romantic talk by those who had not suffered greatly from the famine; it was the desperate talk of those who had. I heard these faint voices rise and bludgeon my mind, voices carried on the wind, drowning out the shallow bells of mediocrity ringing next to my ears as I stood on the threshold. Suddenly I let the daring glimmer of irresponsibility catch in that wind.

'Ching Chong Chinaman.' It's difficult to say why that offends me. In the boys' home I was quick to use my fists when those voices mocked me, but all that I ever hit were shadows and obsessions.

Dinnertimes were worst. Father O'Shea supervised dinner and was as deaf as Terry Galletti, the boy beside me at the table. Father O'Shea read his missal without lifting his head while the boys stuck butter on the ceiling, poured tea into the salt and invented names for me. Terry Galletti was struggling with his spoon. (He suffered from St. Vitus' Dance.) The boys screamed, jumped, danced on the tables, pretended to foam at the mouth like Terry, stretched their eyes with their fingers at me, uttered a gibberish of what purported to be Chinese, or Japanese, or both. Father O'Shea read on.

'You hear them?' I said to Terry.

'What?' he said, his spoon slipping past his chin and into his shirt.

That was such a long time ago. My passport still lies open before me, tempting me to embark on imaginary journeys. The past sits heavily in my stomach. Shan's journal, inextricably entwined in mine, strengthens my fragile sensitivity.

Oh, I admit that I suffered from feelings of persecution. Voices taunted me, shadows pursued me with cleavers. Reason was the only mainstay of my sensitivity. Once the boundaries of reason were crossed, sensitivity ran amuck. The imagination had a secret way through the border. 'Stay away from strong imagination,' the doctor once told me. The imagination always forced me to act. Once that happened, reason collapsed as easily as unstrung chicken wire.

Perhaps this explains why I carry these small slips of yellow paper around with me, neatly sandwiched in contact plastic. They protect me from paranoia. They are my *raison d'être*. I know they are not fiction.

I do not know why I left my father's house that day and made the trip to the town. I do not know how I managed to find a room to stay for the night, waiting for the arrival of the sun the next day and listening to the sterile conversation between a woman and a man through the paper-thin walls. One action simply entailed the next. At dawn I bought a passage on the British ship *Phaeton*, bound for Australia, known only to me then as The South Land.

I cannot remember what was in my mind that dark morning a week later as I packed my small bundle of clothes, my earthenware stove, the two pots I found in the kitchen and the meat-cleaver I used for slaughtering chickens. I was about to leave a coin on the table. The cleaver would prove harmful if I did not pay. Then I told myself that I was finished with such superstitions.

I do remember stealing past my father's room, inhaling the scent he regularly used, and stepping out into the cold air. I glanced once at the huge shape of Tai Mo Shan, exhaled a puff of vapour and shouldered my bundles, which swung clumsily at first on the ends of the stout bamboo pole. Once I got into my rhythmic jog I felt better, the load feeling as light as my heart. For the first time in my life I sensed freedom. I still remember feeling a strange premonition of being in touch with and confident of the future. I was becoming a modern man.

2 JOURNEYS

I do not know when exactly the sounds and voices of the past began to come to me. I like to believe that they coincided with the time I left school and with what I now call my period of irresponsibility.

I was aware that my appearance created around me a desolation, a metaphysical landscape as barren as the Sahara. Perhaps this was due more to my own penchant for isolation than to the boundaries marked out by reality. I saw myself as a foreigner, and this view pushed me into situations where it became fact. At the same time the feeling of being foreign evoked in me an almost obsessive curiosity about what I liked to call 'the secrets of place'. It was in some way connected to the explosion of my sexual life, an internal, masturbatory instinct linked with the need to see, to gaze into the dark, secret places in houses, behind curtains, under covers, sheets, skirts—in short, inside the skull. Thus I became a voyeur.

There was no realization of this at the time. What I felt then seemed to stem from the positive, active attributes of my nature, the powerful, interlinked sensations of freedom and invisibility.

And so it was with these feelings that I embarked on that hot and sunny day for my first job interview. At the employment office I heard the girl take the telephone call:

'Yes, Mr Gold.'

'No, Mr Gold.'

'Yes, Chinese.'

'Right, Mr Gold.'

'Start today?'

'Yes, thank you.'

'Bye, Mr Gold.'

She looked up at me from her desk, her eyes authoritatively searching mine, which were hidden behind thick lenses like tiny crabs in a rock-pool.

'How would you like a job as a storeman? You can start to-day,' she said.

'It isn't a job I would really like ...' I hesitated; yet the idea of returning to the boys' home seemed more repugnant every second. She began putting away the card she was scribbling on, ignoring my desperation.

'But I'll take it,' I said.

'They may not take you on,' she said, her clam-like eyes searching my vulnerability. 'But you can have a go,' she continued, the clams opening, poised in the warm current of air sweeping in from the street. 'It's at Surry Hills.'

I walked there to save on the bus fare. It was a shabby, run-down factory-cum-warehouse. I took the lift up from a dark stairwell. A huge lift with gates at both ends, it moved slowly, smoothly, and arrived on the fourth floor with a slight creak. I opened the gate. I was in an office. A long counter ran along one side. Behind it were three desks and an old-fashioned safe. At the end of the corridor I saw a large room where rows of women sat behind sewing machines, the rhythmic vibration of their machines funnelling down the corridor to me, making the wooden floor hum. The strong, briny smell of dyes wafted down.

A man came towards me from behind the counter. He was a stooping, short man in his fifties. Despite the hot weather, he had on a light-blue cardigan over his white shirt. He also wore a bow tie. He was balding, though thick tufts of hair fell about his ears. He peered at me over a pair of wire-rimmed bifocals.

'My name is Seamus O'Young. I've come about the job.'

'Oh, yes. Vat ist you say your name?'

'Seamus O'Young.'

'Such a funny name for a Chinese.'

'I'm Australian.'

'Really. Hum. You haf some Chinese blod. I can see that. Your fater ist Chinese? Your mutter?'

'I don't know. I'm Australian.'

'That ist unfortunate ... but ve try you out chust the same.'

He motioned me to follow him along the corridor. He walked quickly. I followed him, observing the faces of the women in the rows that I passed. Most of them were middle-aged. They looked like migrants. They glanced up at me without stopping their work, guiding the pieces of material through the machines with their fingers. I noticed one girl with a solemn, attractive face. She did not look at me, but continued working with her agile fingers, her shapely legs close together beneath the machine, bare feet planted firmly on the floor.

'By the vay, my name is Mr Gold.' He brushed past some empty cartons, kicking them into place under a shelf. He led me to the storeroom. It was a room the size of a lavatory. Stacks of cardboard cartons rose to the ceiling. A small window looked out over some roofs. I noticed that the sky was blue.

'This ist vat you haf to do first,' Gold said, indicating the cartons with his bifocals. 'I vant you to tidy this up.' He kicked at some boxes. 'I vill get Carlos to gif you a hand.'

I began to pull down the stacks of cartons. I found the biggest ones and began to put the smaller ones inside each other, in the manner of a Chinese puzzle. Gold stood at the door watching me. He pushed up his spectacles with an index finger. After a few minutes he seemed satisfied that I could do the job. He turned quickly on his heel and walked off, casting his glance here and there among his workers, who all had their heads down over their machines; all except the attractive girl, who was still sitting in an erect position, her head facing forward, unmoved by Gold's light fingers on her shoulders as he passed, a grin registering on his twitching, bifocalled face.

I worked quickly, completing the job in half an hour. I began to explore the room, which seemed twice as big as it had been, with the cartons stacked neatly in the corners. The dank, grey

floor was littered with rat droppings. I searched the edges of
the floor, and the ceiling. There were no holes. I imagined that
Gold would be pleased to have employed a rat-catcher as well.

As my eyes swept along the walls, I noticed a thin stream
of light emerging from one corner. The light flashed once and
then went out. Five minutes later it came on again. I removed
some of the boxes from the corner. The light came from a
hole at about eye-level in the wall. I peered through the hold.
It was the women's lavatory next door. I had a perfect view of
the whole room, since the mirror was in such a position that it
reflected the corners along my wall.

From the cubicle a large women emerged, hoisting up her
undergarments with slow, elephantine movements, pulling her
short sleeves in and out to fan under her arms, adjusting her
brassiere with short snaps of the elastic which made her breasts
bob up and down like buoys in an ocean of fat. Then, without
washing her hands, she put out the light.

At that moment I had the feeling that someone was watching me. I turned around and was confronted with a bull-shaped
man whose neck was as thick as my thigh and whose dark head
was part of his neck, his little eyes bloodshot, the bridge of his
nose sunk into his forehead as though a hatchet had been embedded there for some time.

'You the new bloke? I'm Carlos,' the bull-shaped man said,
extending a paw that shot out of his overalls.

'Seamus O'Young,' I said, noticing the over-excessive grip of
the Spaniard's hand.

'I suppose to help you, but you done it all by yourself.' He
smirked, placing his hand back into the bib of his overalls. 'Mr
Gold think you're a good hand. You listen to me and you get on.'

He shifted some of the cartons round to a position that satisfied him best and then began to list the jobs I was supposed
to do.

'You can scrape the shit off the floor first,' he said, smudg-
ing some of the droppings with his boot. 'Then you can put

mothballs in these cartons and take a stack out to the girls. They tell you what to do next.'

He walked off in the direction of the attractive girl, stopping behind her to joke with the large woman, nodding at the girl's back, the large woman blushing but laughing as though she really enjoyed the joke. I began to scrape up the droppings with the lid of a box.

It was at that moment that I thought I heard a voice deep within me say: 'Compromise and resignation are traits that reach far back into your ancestry. They understood, those people, that freedom is economic, not ideological.' The voice was like a crackling record, scratched with age, or like sound consumed by fire. I heard the roaring of my own hostility.

Towards lunchtime I had cleaned the floor and put handfuls of mothballs in the boxes. Gold came into the storeroom, looked in the boxes and seemed pleased.

'Take them now to Anna. She vill tell you vat next to do,' he said, satisfaction passing over his face like a cloud withdrawing from the sun.

He left without telling me who Anna was. I carried a load of boxes to the door. Behind one of the rows of women I saw the fat lady. By now I felt familiar with her, and there was even a slight superiority in my voice, a power I had never felt before, as I addressed her.

'Who is Anna?' I asked, looking straight into her cow-like face.

She indicated to me with her finger the attractive girl sitting in front of her. With the same movement her finger withdrew to her armpit, giving her strap another tug. Whether it was a good excuse to break from her monotonous work, or whether it was an act of modesty under my staring eyes, it was hard to say. I went up to Anna, timidly this time, watching her eyes follow the rapid needle flicking close to her finger, the lashes moving up and down slowly.

'Where shall I take these?' I asked, shouted, above the din

of the machines. She did not look up or answer. I watched her take the cardigan she was working on off the machine, pick up another one, cut off the tag that said 'Made In China' which was sewn to the collar, pick up another tag from a tin that said 'Golden Textiles', and begin to sew it on. I shouted the question again.

When she had finished this time she looked up at me, then she saw the boxes and pointed to the stacks of cardigans next to her machine. I felt insulted by this rudeness, and sensed my isolation. I felt the vast distance between myself and everyone with whom I came into contact. It was as though I were contagious and others did not want to be contaminated by my foreignness. Yet it was something that I took pleasure in.

I began to pack the boxes with cardigans. I noticed another surge of power rise in me. I felt untouchable.

Carlos came down the aisle and began to help me. He had a smile on his face that made his eyes withdraw into the indentation of his nose.

'Anna's dumb,' he said to me as he bent to pick up an armful of cardigans. As he said that, I looked at her and it dawned on me that her rudeness was an aspect of the affinity between us. She was untouchable, too. The vast desert harboured her voice, had it in safekeeping for ever in its emptiness. Her eyes looked into mine for a second. There was some possibility of communication between us.

An electric bell on the wall began to clang. Instantly the machines stopped, and the women began to reach for bags by the sides of their machines. Carlos dropped the stack of cardigans on to the floor. Anna picked up her handbag, her face now transformed completely, a light smile playing on her lips. She went to the lavatory.

'Lunch,' Carlos said in the unusual silence. I stood there, not knowing what to do. I had brought no lunch. Women drew their chairs up into little groups, sharing their sandwiches, their fruit. Carlos joined them. I made my way to the office. Gold's door was shut. I stepped into the lift and descended, feeling the lightness within myself. A voice said to me, 'Freedom for half an hour. How precious time becomes for the unreflective; for those who are alive and yet are dead!'

When I returned to the factory with a hamburger, Gold was waiting for me. He slid back the gate of the lift and said, 'Next time you vill bring your lunch? It is better this vay. More nourishing. You can have it here.'

He led me into his office, a small cubicle filled with ledgers, overflowing with boxes of cardigans, carpeted with sample books of material.

'Sit down and have your lunch,' he said, offering me a chair. He went out and left his door open. I was sitting in front of his desk, looking up at the two framed law degrees on the walls. Written in florid script, they said:

In the name of the Senate and by
authority of the same
Be it known
That ABRAHAM FEINGOLD ...

As I ate my hamburger before these impressive credentials I saw Gold reflected in the glass, watching me from outside the office, his wire-rimmed bifocals fixed to the back of my head. The bell clanged for the end of lunch.

As the afternoon wore on, I found myself back in the storeroom, preparing more boxes for packing. The sky outside the window was now overcast, and thunder rumbled in the south. As I continued my work I saw the light from my secret peephole come on again, and this time I was drawn to it by the sound of a low humming, an atonal humming that sounded to me like Indian or Chinese music. I had prepared a spot for myself around the peephole so that I was shielded by cartons practically on all sides. In the safety of my position I would not be surprised by anyone coming into the storeroom.

As I focused my eye on the mirror of the lavatory I saw Anna come from the toilet cubicle. She was looking at herself in the mirror, brushing back her dark hair with one hand, making the strange humming noise, walking backwards and forwards beside the mirror, all the while staring and smiling at herself. Then she bent down and began to remove her stockings, rolling them down past her ankles and then drawing them off, placing them in her handbag. Then she undid her blouse, and I saw the tops of her breasts, pale in the neon glow. She splashed some water on to her face and chest and then, without doing up her blouse, began to fumble in her handbag. She took out a lipstick and a small compact, and began to do her face.

I felt myself become excited, not by her state of undress but by the way she was applying her lipstick, her mouth formed into an oval kiss, her eyes lit up by the redness of her lips. As she applied the lipstick puffs of vapour came from her mouth and were registered on the mirror, so that she had to move to another spot, which soon became misted. I became almost uncontrollably excited by this movement of hers, this itinerant kissing of her own image, this vaporous emission that clouded my view of her face, the muffled oracle from the well of her mouth. I was entranced by the atonal music rising from within the solitude of a deaf-mute.

Suddenly I heard a sound behind me. I was so preoccupied that I had not heard Carlos come into the storeroom. He was standing almost directly at my back, having removed some cartons, and was watching me.

'You're a bloody pervert, O'Young,' he said, a mixture of malice and satisfaction in his grin. I felt immediately impotent, my power wrested away by the bull-like thrust of his head. He began to push back the cartons, blocking the peephole.

'I'll ask Mr Gold for some putty,' he said as he motioned me to carry out the stack of cartons I had left in the corner.

I was glad the day was coming to an end. Carlos began to order me about as though he owned the place. I was glad, too, that the rain was finally falling, cloaking the streets in sheets of water. I looked forward to merging into the sea of workers returning home, feeling myself swept along by the stream of shapes filtering into the darkness.

Two days later I quit the job. I told Gold that I had won a lottery and that I had no need to work any longer. He did not believe me, of course; but I couldn't tell him that I had quit because Carlos had blocked up my peephole, that there was no longer any point in staying.

Gold's parting words to me were: 'So you von a lottery. I didn't see your name in the papers. Just like that. So you vin just like that, and you vant to go. You know, ven I put the position in the employment office I ask specially for a Chinese. You know, a Chinese because they have respect. They verk hard. But I see you are not like that. You are just the same as the rest. No respect, no principles, vat I vant vith you ...'

While he was still talking, I slipped into the lift, closed the gate, and pressed the button for the ground floor.

Here are the realities:

1. The ship was not as big as the ones I have seen since.

2. The master of the vessel was a red-haired Englishman by the name of Morrison.

3. He demanded all the money I had for the passage, saying that I would more than double that amount in my first two weeks of gold-digging.

As soon as I set foot on the deck of that ship I realized that I had sold myself for the idea of the journey. My freedom was shackled to a space below the deck. The men slept in rows next to their bundles in the bowels of the ship. Though some of the faces were familiar to me, there were no hints of recognition.

As soon as we boarded the ship we were herded below decks. Some of us, unused to the steps, fell down on to the hard floor. Huge iron grates were placed across the opening. In the semi-darkness we heard the water lapping against the side of the ship, the creaking timbers, the clump of footsteps above us. We waited for hours, solemnly regarding each other, saying little. The hold grew hot in the midday sun. Shafts of light sank into our midst. In these hazy columns men stretched, squatted on their heels, waiting for motion to weigh anchor from the sea of time, harnessing their trepidation, impatient for the journey of their lives.

Suddenly there was a lurch. The ship heeled over and we heard water rushing down the side of the hull. There was a flapping of canvas, shouts in a strange language. Bizarre, this experience of China receding from the faces of her men, smiles breaking out on their lips, memories stored away for the future.

I am already in a foreign land. The men look glumly at the hatch and the grate, staring at the same section of mast, the changing colours of the sky, the clouds. Almost every swell carries up the acrid fumes of urine. Some men are beginning to retch, the fishermen among us laughing. There are the sounds of spray on wood and canvas. Throughout the hold there is also a perfume of tea, becoming now a nauseating smell, from the wooden boxes stacked high above our heads, tied to stanchions with tarred rope.

Night; and the men light small fires in their stoves and share out rice and dried fish. I hear my stomach growl. I have brought no food, but the nausea is pitching around inside of me. At one lurch of the ship a trickle of vomit creeps towards my bundle along the cracks in the floor. We are so close to one another that I am unable to move it. My bundle soaks up the trickle. I begin to heave, my body divorced from my mind by a glacial sweat. Strange how easy it becomes to experience death. My neighbour, a bald-headed old man, nudges me and gives me some dried fish which he has soaked in lemon juice.

'Gnaw on that,' he says.

My teeth sink into the rubbery fish, feeling it come apart into slivers. The lemon juice cools the hot sourness in my throat. My nausea fades.

We sleep head to toe on the hard floor, my face inches away from a pair of yellow soles, the skin emitting a soft reflection of the flickering light from someone's stove, like a pair of giant mushrooms caught springing up in the dark forest by a sunbeam flitting through leaves. I think of my mother's feet, rotting in the earth. In a few years the bones would be unveiled, great elongated toes curling back to the heel. How strange it is to think of the beauty of small, bound feet encased in embroidered silk when I remember her painful walk! And now those feet are destined to become archaeological curiosities, reminders of an exotic dynasty.

It is now early in the morning. Light is beginning to filter through the grating. I have slept well, even with the continuous pitching and yawing of the ship. My days of training in the temple have prepared me well. Once the self is sublimated, adjustment and compromise become easy. 'Beware of too headstrong an imagination,' the monks had warned.

With a crashing and squealing sound, the grates are removed. We are allowed on deck.

How warm the sun feels as I lurch upwards out of the hold! At first it is difficult for my eyes to focus. Gradually I can see the pale wooden decking, the tarred ropes and stays, stretching far above me to the masts and spars. I walk shakily along the length of the ship. Others are doing the same, trying to get some life back into their legs. The ship seems to be moving more quickly today, or was it only my imagination wanting to speed up my journey? But my instinct told me not to heed the imagination, to distil the truth from observation and not let the imagination race on ahead, arriving at the destination before this journey had taken its course.

As I reflected on this I began to see a particular truth emerging from my experience. I began to realize that the imagination sought to emphasize my difference, that my observations set

me apart from the others because the imagination had a habit
of fictionalizing them; and the truth was that, in order to survive this journey, the perils ahead in this land to the south, it
was necessary not to be different but to throw myself into the
experience and act as the others did.

In reality the ship is moving sluggishly, a sodden log
half-submerged in the waves. The crew stare at us, speaking in
strange monotones, laughing now and again. We wander about
like dazed ants. I am aware of their different appearance, the
clothes they wear; yet their physical and facial characteristics
do not seem so different from those of the Manchurians and
Siberians I have met on my journeys to the coast. Perhaps these
people are of a fairer complexion. Our people, who are main-
ly from Kwangtung province, are short and thin; but there is a
Shanghainese among us who would be taller than most of these
Englishmen. This Shanghainese is somewhat of an anomaly
among us.

I lean at the port rail and watch the sea taking great gulps
at the ship, never swallowing it, but slapping at it with foam.
Sometimes a big wave slides the ship down on the palm of its
hand, and when we are at the bottom I imagine seeing Tai Mo
Shan, the mountain of mist, behind me, and I think of my father sitting in his room. I wonder whether he is aware of my
departure, of my absence from the periphery of his life.

At midday we are given some rice and a kind of biscuit,
which would remain our staple diet for the months ahead. A
sailor in a heavy blue jacket gives us the unboiled rice from a
sack which he has placed on the deck. I fill my pockets with
the rice, and as the grains slip through my fingers I am able to
sift out several wriggling worms which I fling into the sea. I am
handed a biscuit. I look at it uncomprehendingly, as the others
do, sceptical of its ability to sustain life. We are herded back to
the hold. The steps are drawn up behind us.

Upon my return to the semi-darkness, I noticed immediately
that the old man, my neighbour in the night, had not moved

from his position. He was lying on his side, a stream of mucus and vomit issuing from his nose and mouth. As I decanted some water from a bucket and began to wash his face, I noticed his shallow breathing. He smiled weakly at me. It was my turn to offer him food, but he refused the biscuit, he said he wasn't hungry. I boiled some rice and forced him to eat a few grains. I needed to get him out on to the deck.

From the heat of his forehead and the sweat pouring from his face, I deduced that his illness was more than mere seasickness. I went below the grate and began to shout to the sky above. It was useless. My throat became hoarse, and I choked from the smoke that was now beginning to fill the hold as the men lit up their stoves. There was a lot of murmuring.

Suddenly the tall Shanghainese rose from among his pots and came towards me, suggesting, in his resonant dialect, that I could stand on his shoulders and perhaps reach the grate and attract the attention of the crew. It was difficult. The rolling of the ship seemed to increase, and more than once I fell off, landing among the cooking pots of a spidery old fisherman. Curses strung like fish mingled with our shouts for help. After some minutes a face peered down at us, a big, bearded, angry face. I babbled at it with my useless language. The face disappeared.

Back in my corner, the old man was smiling at me through the smoke.

I believe I heard a voice shouting to me for help during that long period of destitution when I was without a job. It called to me a few moments ago.

I am lying in a park, my face shielded from the strong sun by the branches of a tree. I am losing my sense of time. Two old men are sitting with their backs against the trunk. Between them they have a bottle of wine. One takes long swallows from the bottle; the other seems to be asleep. The one who is drinking offered me a sandwich about half an hour ago. It was a ham sandwich. I ate it with great bites and swallows, my stomach seizing the mouthfuls, growling.

Under another tree they are making a commercial. A girl stands in front of the camera in a long fur coat. She stands there, sweating, smiling. A tall, fair-haired man next to her pulls out a packet of cigarettes. He draws one, lights it up, inhales deeply. The girl, sweating, smiling, breathes in the fumes of his exhalation.

The voice of the old man who is drinking from the bottle: 'Greta Garbo tits, mate.' He takes a swig from the bottle. 'Wish I had a fag.'

I looked across to the European trees in the hot-house haze. The harsh light; some musty sadness of landscapes of the twenties and thirties; the smell of soured wine; a millennium of space weeping for Europe; the way a butterfly opens and closes its wings in a bizarre display of colour and movement. Rampant materialism. Shit, I was hungry.

'Watch for the butt, mate.'

'How about free samples?'

'Not you, you ol' bugger.'

'Stink. That's what it is, stink.'

'Fuckin' bastids.'

'Willie, you awake, you ol' bastid?'

He shakes the man who seems to be asleep. The man falls over in a heap.

'He's not breathing', the ol' bugger.'

My fingers in my pocket, the girl sweating, the voice shouting for help. I run towards the camera, shouting for help. I feel the warm glare of the big lights behind me. My fly is undone. The woman in the fur coat looks at me, smiling. I'm trying to say something at the top of my voice ...

But my face is being warmed now by the sun that has passed over the branches. Yes, that's what I would like to do, say something to her; but what? The old man shakes the heap. He is crying, big tears rolling down his face from his red eyelids. He looks at me; he is blaming me for Willie's death. I saw the distrust in his eyes when I pulled a book from my paper bag.

'You bloody Chink. Garn. Go back to where you come from.'

I tried to help. I even thought of running in front of the lights and the camera. But I couldn't, you see. I had this book on my chest. Yes, a book. It stopped up my imagination. I couldn't move because of the jam-up of words. Poverty had no racial barriers; but the book, yes, that was it, the book. He hated me because of it. That was my first lesson in learning how to be ignorant. It was a form of adjustment. I got along better then.

So I had a secret vice. So I hung around bookstores. I read what I could and when I could. I used to get kicked out. So I stole books. But what did these pieces of knowledge mean? What were these chunks of dreams, secreted away in my duffel-bag? I was safe in a book, looking inside. I was constructing a huge puzzle without head or tail, a puzzle that was continually expanding. I was trying to order my world. Strands of reality hung off it. Experiences were true and untrue. All the time this voice was calling for help, telling me that I could fix it up, if only I could help; participate; act.

Strange then, my impulse to sell the books to the second-hand dealer. Strange how light I felt, discarding all those experiences, my mind wandering already, down to the station, looking for the right train, wanting to journey backwards because there was order in the past; historical sequences, completed puzzles. Strange how glad I felt handing over the money at the ticket counter, meeting the stare of the ticket seller instead of looking down at the brass tray inset in the stained wooden counter under the grille.

The trains. Coming in. Going out. Corridors of time. I enter the compartment feeling slightly cold. I stare out the window. It is dark outside. Trains are luxurious, like foyers of grand hotels. Comfort, warmth, digging in for the long journey, staring out all the time. Not like buses. Journeys in buses are too short. In buses people communicate too much with their eyes. It is a less private, more inquiring form of transport. People used to stare at me a lot. I imagined what they were thinking. I developed theories about the stare. Some were gazes; flickering, momentary, unpractised. Others ranged from aggression to curiosity. Ignorant people tended to stare longer, unselfconsciously. Usually I imagined their minds to be clear, a fairly barren landscape with a few rock-like opinions. Honest, clever people tended not to stare at all, but sometimes I caught them stealing a look. Then their faces would become self-righteous. People with pretensions were the worst. They usually belonged to clubs. This is what they think:

'There's a bloody Chong. He doesn't belong to our club. He spoils the look of the club. Get rid of him. If he's allowed in there will be millions of them. They don't speak the language. They don't mix.'

People with pretensions are always under threat. They are unused to handling ideas.

Trains are different. Trains are private. There is only a small group of people in my immediate surroundings. Not like buses, where I have to pay the driver and walk down the aisle in front of the whole audience as though it was a freak show. In trains there is no mob instinct. The train moves slowly out of the station. Nobody watches me. I am on a floating island of metaphors, jamming up the present. The past banks up like a tidal wave.

I am having a nightmare. I am not in this dark vessel, moving through the ocean, the moon appearing huge, like a lantern a small boy carries, tied to the end of a stick. The night brings me familiar smells; flowers that smell like tea, the sweetish odour of nightsoil, the salt-bearing wind from the sea, the sharp flavour of the tobacco old men smoke; familiar sounds; of water drawn from a distant well, the steady creak of the windlass, the wooden bucket knocking at the sides. Already I feel the magnetic pull of the land, the pleasure of waking from the nightmare upon a bed, the commencement of the daylight hours of the dream.

Next to me the old man coughs and turns over, the sighing of the waves now in time with his laboured breathing. I feel a kind of heaviness clamp down over my chest.

In the dark the train hardly seems to be moving. An occasional light flips by, bringing the countryside to me; the lights are crouching under huge gums which are like dark blankets of cloud. The train slows down at a siding. I see a farmhouse, peer into its window. A family of three are having dinner, the table laid with a red-checked tablecloth. Jack, Edna and I are having dinner. Not knowing what to say, I am stuffing my mouth with warm potato. Jack, still wearing his hat, is munching slow mouthfuls, saying in his detached voice, 'Eat slowly, boy.' The train scrapes and shuffles on.

All through the night the magnetic pole draws me on in my tube of steel. In the morning the red sun reaches up over bare hills, and the moon hangs undecided, low on the other side. Then, like a mirror in a compact, it is returned to the handbag. With a click, it disappears behind the hills that are still dark and cool from the night. The woman opposite me sighs, makes a face into her mirror and puts it back into her handbag. She gets up unsteadily, doing a slow waltz to the lavatory.

The journey continues towards the state border, the train at a crawling pace, my head aching now with the hunger, and I noticed that every time I got hungry the voice in me became more insistent. It said: 'Eliminate the self and the will becomes stronger.' The voice is Chinese. It comes to me crackling and scratching like a short-wave broadcast.

I go to the lavatory and the white dial on the door says vacant, so I push it open; and the woman is there, sitting over the bowl, her dress up around her waist, her hands under it, her stockings rolled down, her heavily made-up face pale and startled by my entry. I close the door quickly, just in time to hear her say 'Oh'; something heavy is suddenly thrust against it on the other side, and I watch the dial click into engaged. I start back to my seat along the corridor, and the view of the land out the window is suddenly different: harsh brown and red soil, gnarled trees, the sun glaring above. I wait for a while in my seat. The woman does not return. I do not see her again.

When I go to the lavatory this time it is empty. The seat is still warm. As I evacuate my bowels I feel a tremendous power surge up within me. The turd falls straight down the hole and on to the tracks, which run like the frames of a film beneath me. The outside world receives my offering; poor, desiccated shards of grass and seeds, dry like the drought-stricken land. I am warm and flushed, clean and strong. Beneath my gaze, there is the clarity of real things, unhidden, unenclosed, unpuzzling.

The train eases into the station in the small town. I have arrived, but I do not feel that I have arrived, the train having moved so slowly that there seemed to have been an infinite regression. It is the end of the day. There is a deathly silence when I step on to the platform. I can feel the cool air on my body. The train crackles and creaks like an old film.

I remember the town well enough. It sits at the foot of the hills near some old gold mines. I walk along the road to the south. Two miles along that road I turn left and follow a long dusty track which dips and winds through large pools of white sand. It is cold now, and the darkness makes the sand look like snow. The track leads into a pine forest. The trees, close together, tower over me. Pine needles obscure the track. I feel my way through the opening, and I soon see a light. The house sits squat on the ground, white in the semi-darkness, a light from the window casting its warmth over the stony ground littered with pine cones. The thought of someone's privacy makes me feel uneasy. I breathe in the night air. I knock twice. There is a shadow beneath the door.

Soon the moon disappeared behind a darker sky, which had been sliding like a black lid under it. The wind gusts increased and made the sails snap and ruffle, while the yards swung around and strained, the canvas luffing, whipping and bucking like the flanks of an angry dragon. Suddenly there were shouts and clamouring on deck, and the ship began to yaw, wallowing in the bigger waves which I now imagined were beginning to break before reaching the stern. Then I heard the blasts of rain, splattering on the deck like rice being threshed on wooden boards. The men hung on to whatever was not rolling or sliding in the hold. Since there were so many of us in such a confined space, space that was becoming dangerous for us, the men in the middle began to hang on to the ones at the side, who in turn were grasping firmly the ropes restraining the chests of tea. And so we felt as one, linked to each other and to our produce in a foreign ship upon a foreign sea, the vision of a gold mountain melting away to nothing: in its place, the green walls and cliffs of tons of water.

Suddenly a huge wave cracked over the ship, knocking everything down with its mighty force. The ship lurched and listed dangerously, and the port side must have caught the water and ploughed in momentarily, slowing the ship with a jolt, slewing it round so that the next wave, which was luckily a smaller one, slapped at the stern and buoyed the ship up for that necessary half-second. We were standing almost on the side of the hull now, the sea streaming in through the hatch like a waterfall. Then the ship flung itself back, and at that moment the ropes holding the tea chests broke, and the boxes of tea, each weighing a great deal, crashed on top of us. Some of them

broke open. Men were drowning in tea. The big Shanghainese
struggled from among this mass of bodies and, like a leviathan,
surfaced and spread his arms wide, preventing the other chests
from falling.

During all this confusion I had been flung aft by the impact
of the first wave. I wedged myself between huge coils of hemp
which cushioned me from the falling crates. I was holding on to
the old man, cradling his head in my arms. He seemed to have
lost consciousness.

Just as it had begun, the storm eased, and the ship stopped
rolling. I was suddenly aware of the stench coming from my
own clothes. I was covered in excrement and vomit from the
buckets that had been rolling over me, and I began to bring up
the little food I had swallowed an hour before. Gradually the
men stirred, rising and falling again among the debris, holding
their heads and limbs, checking the injuries they had sustained.
Nobody spoke.

Gradually the sky lightened and the sea became calm, and
lying in that stinking, foul pit we heard voices above, and the
grate was lifted, a makeshift ladder descending like a snake.
Slowly the men began to climb up, moving only an arm or a
leg, like damaged caterpillars crawling back up a tree.

The Shanghainese and I carried the old man up on deck
and laid him on a pile of sodden canvas. The crew kept away
from us, probably because of our smell. Then one man, a short,
thick-set fellow in an oilskin approached us and inspected the
old man, using sign language to ask, I presumed, whether he
is dead. When I indicated that he was still breathing, he reluc-
tantly signalled to two others and they carried him away with
them to the forward area of the ship.

I stood at the rail amazed at the calm of the sea and noticed
the clarity of the world, how the sky was washed clean, how
the sun which, although it was shining without warmth, was
magnifying everything around me; and I seemed to be looking
through a piece of glass and was glad of this experience, noting

in my mind that this seeing was part of the progression into
eternity.

Edna Grove opened the door, peered at me with her short-sight-
ed eyes. She stood for some time at the door, beside the brass
plate that said *Twin Groves*, looking into the darkness and then
at me, not seeing, not recognizing me. I studied her face closely.
Her hair had gone grey. It was hanging loose down her back,
and as she bent forward to look deeper into the blackness the
silver strands tumbled over her shoulder. It was long, like a
horse's mane, straight and fine. Her eyes were still lively and
blue, but around them some wrinkles had gathered like sheep
tracks leading to twin dams of clear blue water.

She stood there, looking at me in her old blue dressing-gown.
I had forgotten that she was a good deal shorter than I was. My
dark shadow passed over her eyes. There was a spark, and suddenly her lined face lit up like so much kindling.

'Seamus,' she said softly. 'Seamus, my darling boy!' she exclaimed, stepping outside and holding me by the shoulders.
Then she grabbed my face and kissed me, a little roughly, on
the cheek, and drew back looking at me, a bit embarrassed.
'Welcome home,' she said.

'Hullo, Eddie,' I said, smiling at her confusion over the time
and distance I had brought back to her. 'Eddie' was the name
I had always called her. She was never 'mother' to me, though
I could have called her that through affection. The feelings I
knew to be associated with that word I reserved for the mytho-
logical person I held at the back of my mind, connected to me
only through a glimmer of consciousness: when some aspect
of the land reminded me of my own emptiness, or the sighing
of the wind told me that she, listening to the same sound of
the wind, must have thought about me and wondered if I were
alive.

'Come in, dear boy, come in,' Edna said, taking me by the arm and dragging me through the narrow doorway, our hips touching as I drew back and allowed her through. As she walked on ahead of me I saw how youthful she still looked from behind, the dressing-gown outlining her figure, the fine silver hair streaming down her back, and I thought how the ravages of alcohol had done nothing to her sprightly walk, her quick movements, and the erect way in which she held herself. She led me through the hallway and into the living-room. I saw immediately into her life, and recognized something of how I knew her to be in the past.

The room was like the cabin of a storm-tossed ship. Everywhere there were empty bottles, old newspapers, knitting-needles stuck into balls of wool. Her dinner plate was on the table, two chop bones like ancient relics on a huge porcelain crucible, the knife and fork crossed beneath it. Near the window there were some old suitcases lying open; in them a jumble of clothes, a flowery dress spilling out, slough of a past fancy. While I was gazing at the room, the huge fire cracked and spat embers on to the old carpet, burning little holes in it so that there was a mosaic of black and red jewels decorating the floor.

'My, you're looking well,' Edna said, seating herself on the sofa, staring up at me. I shifted my weight from one foot to the other.

'Oh, do sit down. You're at home now,' she said with a deep throaty laugh reminiscent of one of Marlene Dietrich's rare laughs.

I sat down next to her and looked about me as she filled two glasses with brandy and offered one to me.

'I hope you like brandy,' she said. 'We have nothing else.'

I wondered who besides her the 'we' referred to, but refrained from following that up, and took the glass from her with a shaky hand, hers pausing as she relinquished it to me, as though she thought twice about giving it to me; or perhaps she was just being careful not to spill it.

'Thank you,' I mumbled, immediately bringing it to my lips saying 'Cheers' in the middle of a swallow. The warm fluid loosened the scaffolding around the conflicting feelings that were building up in me.

'Now, tell me about yourself,' she said, pulling her dressing-gown close around her body as she savoured the last drops of brandy from her already empty glass.

So I talked about myself, explained my long silence, told her about my experience, all these glossed over with a mixture of self-consciousness and self-effacement, keeping close to the proprieties, skirting safely around dangerous lacunae that didn't belong to the image I was creating of myself: gaps that if strung together would have been truer to what I am, because essentially I am a being hedging around nothingness, my centre arid, desolate, unfulfilled.

I noticed that Edna was not really listening to my voice, but was looking around as though alert to some ultrasonic disturbance. She poured herself another drink, searched for and found another world she had left, her face sinking into some dark corner of her soul.

I became aware of the futility of my talk, my voice a soporific drone, and suddenly Edna interrupted me, saying in a hoarse voice, 'Make the journey! Make the journey!' Then she smiled at me, and I didn't know whether she was being deliberately enigmatic or aphoristically wise, or even striving to be impressive. But I had a great respect for age, and thought no more of it than as advice gained and given perhaps too easily on the vaporous edge of alcohol.

Then there was silence, and I noticed that she had lapsed back into some thought of hers. And I noticed something else there in the room, piled on the sofa next to me, lying on the floor, on the windowsill, under chairs, and lying open on the sideboard.

Books. Hundreds of books. I had never been so aware of them in the past. Their silence was punctuated by the explosions in the fire, the light flickering over their pages. A distant generator pounded out its rhythms. Books. My lungs filled like sails and my heart took on the steady rhythm. I felt myself moving, slowly, into another world.

'And if it's all right I would like to stay for a couple of weeks,' I said to her.

She broke off her thought and swam back towards me, her face still bearing the traces of the other communication.

'I'd like you to stay as long as you like,' she said, getting up from the sofa smiling and reaching across a stack of books for her cigarettes. 'Would you like a cigarette?' she asked me, her fingers fumbling with the catch on the gold case. I declined. 'I like a cigarette when I'm alone, you know,' she continued, tapping the cigarette expertly on the back of the case. 'It's ... well ... it's sort of ... company, you understand.'

I nodded as I watched her light it, scraping the match towards her cigarette held in the corner of her mouth.

'We never smoked, Jack and I,' she said, exhaling a cloud. 'But now ...' She broke off, taking another puff. Then she forgot what she was going to say, or perhaps implied that I shouldn't know; and I thought of the 'we' she used, and concluded that the spirit of Jack was still there, in the kitchen, sitting hunched at the table beside the wood stove, cleaning his shotgun.

Edna looks towards the kitchen, and there is a fire in her lined face.

The old men are coming on deck now, calling upon the 'fung' and the 'shui', the wind and the water. They pray for fair winds to prevail and for the waters to be calm. There is a lot of shrieking and howling. They light pieces of prayer-paper and send them into the breeze. The crew are bewildered. They watch the ceremony with respect; but then they try to stop the paper-burning. Already several burning particles have drifted towards the lower sails. The old men are cursing this interference.

Something in me does not fit my feelings. I respect the old men, but am embarrassed by this ceremony. We are sailing to a Christian land. I am as sceptical of the religion of our people as I am of Christianity; but I am not so sceptical that I do not even admit the testing of all religious experience.

I learnt this from a foreigner who called himself a missionary, a man who spoke our language and visited our village before the disturbances forced him to leave. It was something I learnt in spite of him. I say this because he was a most uncompromising man, a man given to rages and violence when I questioned him about his religion. (He was Portuguese, and had a hot temper.) He used to instruct me on his dogma. I listened to him, but was not willing to believe. Most of the time he attacked our ancestor worship, Buddhist and Taoist beliefs. He was very unpopular in the village. He said to me once while we were taking the sun in the garden behind my father's house:

'Shan,' he said, looking me squarely in the eye, 'Shan, you have to pray for yourself to save your own soul. Forget this family worship. You have to do it alone.' And then he blurted out some French, which he was fond of using in order to emphasize a point: 'Découragez les autres,' he said to me, wagging his index finger beneath my nose.

He told me about his god, a prophet who was nailed to a beam of wood by the unbelievers. I have heard such stories about people in our own land. Above all, it seemed to me that his was a philosophy of suffering. I was not prepared to believe in a philosophy of suffering. It was fatalistic, self-destructive, hallucinatory. Yet I found it attractive. I saw in it a possible explanation for the grain of sand that was irritating my heart; my basic cynicism, my radical association with chaos, my irresponsibility and rejection of my filial duty (that great Confucian ideal). In this philosophy of suffering, there was at least a dramatic, emotional force that was above chaos, appearing on the other side, as it were, of the Buddhist calm; a force that made possible an active, participatory suffering, full of lightning and thunder of vast, cataclysmic proportions, a whole universe of weeping that generated more faith.

On the other hand, the Portuguese seemed to be on a mission of dividing and conquering. I had yet a lot to learn about the philosophy of suffering.

I do not know what it is that makes me run. Each day I run along the tracks criss-crossing the pine forests near the house. Nothing about the landscape is familiar to me. I cannot remember that I spent years of my childhood here. Everything has grown over, the past covered by a new skin. As I run over the dead pine needles and feel the cones scrunch under my soles I am aware of another past, a deeper one embedded in the soil. Something seems to form the beginning of a whole history here, and I am somewhere along it.

I ran, driven by two demons; the demon of the body, the continuous present, and the demon of the mind, which harboured the other life, intent only on seeing into the past. My senses became sharp, the mind's eye focusing as it had never done before. Sometimes the warmth of the morning garnished my run with distinctive smells. One place in the forest offered a smell of Goldfaber pencils, another place a smell of old books, the kind with rough, uncut pages. Along one section of the track which leads away from the house into the hills, and which stops abruptly at a huge boulder, there was a strong smell of ink, a sweetish smell which I suspected emanated from a small creek and its attendant undergrowth. These smells, for some reason, always made me hungry.

One morning I ran twice as fast back the way I had come. I reached the back door panting, sweating, my head spinning, feeling light but strong. Easing the shrieking muscles in my legs, I walked very slowly to my room at the end of the hallway.

Passing Edna's room, involuntarily turning my head to peer through the gap between the half-open door and wall, I saw her standing naked with her back to me. In the ray of light coming through her window, I caught sight of the reflection of her body in the mirror, and saw the swathe of silver hair enmeshing her thighs before the wall interposed itself. I went to my room confused, unsure if it were Edna that I had seen, the vision returning to me of her face gazing at her body; and suddenly I understood her suffering, and a wave of compassion swept over me clearing everything before it except my hunger. So I walked back along the passageway to the kitchen. Her door was shut tight.

Sometimes I went out before midday to gather cones for the fire. While I put the cones in a basket I would glimpse from the corner of my eye a movement in the forest, a dark shape crossing an opening from behind the branches, crossing the dark floor of the forest a long distance away.

I am learning English. It is a strange language. I am learning it in spite of myself. When I hear the masts and ropes creak, when I hear the soughing waves rush eagerly towards the ship, when I see the mane-like spindrift trailing like a mad woman's hair, I utter English sibilants, like an old hag without teeth, muttering into the wind. (How does one translate 'sibilants' into English?) Yes, I'm learning it in spite of myself. In fits. And starts.

It did not take me long to determine that the English are addicted to a principle called service. They are born and bred for it. It is like our filial duty, only they serve masters unquestioningly and loyally. Given half a chance, the average Englishman, like our Mandarins, cannot resist the idea of being served, of being superior to the servant: and, in the case of the Englishman, especially if the servant is of another race. All this without a thought to the fact that he himself has pledged his life to the service of someone above himself. And so it goes. There is always someone above, right up to the king. Above the king there is God and country. And so it turns full circle. Of course the king will never have to serve a beggar. There is God in between. This God will do the duty of serving the poor and the destitute. At least this is what the Portuguese Jesuit told me. (He was very much against the English.)

There was one particular Englishman in the crew who seemed to be fairly important. He gave orders on deck and was instantly obeyed. It was to this man that I applied the theory of service, helping him clear the deck of debris after the storm, removing a torn sail from a spar that had fallen. It turned out that he was the ship's carpenter, and it was from him that I learnt how to craft and shape the English language. It did not take him long to see that I was capable of certain tasks and that I was quick to understand his instructions. He instructed me in the slow, deliberate way of seamen, using signs and gestures, restricting my tasks to simple repetitive ones and gradually increasing what I had to do to avoid mistakes. After a few weeks I had learnt the rudiments of the language, and the fundamentals of seamanship, the two being quite similar in my mind, marking a deliberate course over roughly charted seas of bountiful metaphors and conspiring adjectives.

And so I earned the privilege of being the spokesman for my people. Learning this language for practical reasons, I was afraid that I had now begun to place more emphasis on survival than on ideals and adventure. Was this one of the far-reaching effects of the search for gold? Did the ideal of gold, which is at the very foundation of the Chinese mind, mean that there was nothing beyond materialism in life? Was my mother's body laid waste because of its immersion in the acidity of this thought? I felt my loyalties being torn apart, and wished that my mind had been trained merely in the school of service.

Sometimes Edna would come with me to gather pine cones and wood. She always wore a cape, no matter how hot the day. She would walk with me and talk about books, telling me how I ought to read this or that, and sometimes she would bring a book with her, under her cape. Finding a shady tree she would sit down and read to me in a clear voice passages from the book that she liked. I listened carefully, and I would feel a desire to read the book. Yet something held me back.

I had not read anything since I came here. I felt that there was a certain power in books, a power that drew me into them, something over which I had no control. Gradually, what I read would congeal in my head and certain sentences and phrases would recur, fixing and prescribing my behaviour according to the positioning of the words.

One day I spoke to Edna about this anxiety. We were walking through the pine forest, I with my basket and she with her book which she held under her cape. In my basket was an old box camera I had found inside the cupboard in my room. I was putting the film cartridge in it when I told her about this power certain words had over me, as though voices were guiding me along some secret path. I was afraid that I was becoming obsessed. Edna looked at me, her bright eyes flicking glances at my camera from her lined face.

'So you hear them too.' She sighed. 'I'm sure it is just the effects of this place, of its isolation. I wouldn't worry too much about it. I hear them and I put it down to this. Though I do have another theory.'

'What is it?' I asked, intrigued, peering down at the rectangular glass in which she now appeared, her back to me.

'Well, you know how in childhood books can trigger off the imagination so that in the end you don't take too much notice of the text?'

I didn't know what she meant, but I nodded anyway.

'What I mean is that when a child reads a fairy-tale for example, he or she is really writing the book in the subconscious.

Textual images become experiences which the child has created. There is nothing with which to compare them ... am I making myself clear?'

Not in the least; but Edna fascinated me. She had never spo-
ken this way before.

'As you get older,' she continued, 'your own experiences
become more important, and you compare them with those
presented in books. Your imagination, your freedom to create,
becomes restricted by the omniscient author, so that myths and
tales seem to lose their freshness. The primary source of the
imagination has been sullied.'

I was beginning to understand. If I were a primitive man, an
Aboriginal, life would be part of the imagination, and not vice
versa.

Edna bent to pick up a cone.

'Books can set off moods and ideas, though giving them direction becomes increasingly difficult the more books you read.
You are really exhausting the potential within yourself.'

I know. There was fear and trembling in me; the anxiety of
another's influence. But then Edna made it all clear to me.

'These voices that you hear,' she said, sitting down on a large
rock, 'are the accumulation of the imaginations of all your pre-
decessors. You are picking up signals reaching you from well
beyond your childhood, far back from your ancestry. You are
listening to the primary sources of the imagination of your race.
Molecules of their ideals, their ethics, have trickled through in
the forming of your genes. You will have to test their influence
on your imagination and your emotions. These words you hear
are the cache which is your legacy, iron filings sticking to the
magnet ... That's my theory.'

Could my genetic make-up be a legacy of history? Did my
racial characteristics inform my memory with a past beyond
my own which surfaced from the unconscious? I needed something substantial to guide me; a sign, a written word.

Edna hitched up her cape and I snapped her picture. (She

looked like an exotic bird about to take off from the rock.) Her theory had opened up a channel in my mind through which I made contact with the prepotent past. The real and the abstract had already begun to merge: I had a craving for a bowl of rice.

When we went back to the house I picked up an armful of Edna's books and went into my bedroom. I read and read, the words forming patterns in my mind, until I began to dream.

I saw myself reading, lying on the bed, three or four open books around me. It was the way I had always read, with three or four books open. I jump from one book to another, catching the mood from one and then linking up to another. After a while, passages from different books interconnect. I have then a good picture of several interlinked worlds as I read, the momentum generated by each carrying me through them. Different worlds open up. I inhabit all of them.

I was reading in this way. My head felt hot, as though I had a fever. My stomach gurgled with hunger. I got up from my books, went to the mirror above the old dresser, saw myself in it, saw a flushed face, an elongated head, ears protruding. I had completely forgotten the way I looked. I was looking at another person. I could not believe that I was staring at myself, standing there in a checked shirt, my hair longish and curling under my ears. I arranged myself in a different position. I stood sideways, trying to look at my profile. Is this how others see me? I tilted the mirror. I straightened it. My features were definitely Asiatic. What determines Asiatic features? The form of the skull. The fold of the eyelids. The colour of the skin. Is my skin really yellow? It does not seem so different from Edna's skin, which I saw reflected in her mirror. Perhaps it was the light.

I pushed the dresser towards the window and pulled back the curtains. I tilted the mirror again. Without the wall to limit the angle of tilt, the mirror was suddenly released from its hinges and fell to the floor. I stood there, looking out the window at the pines. For several moments all was still. A magpie made a sound like spittle in a flute. I walked round to the back of the dresser. The mirror lay in three large pieces on the wooden floor. I saw myself standing in three places above it.

As I picked up the pieces I noticed that the wooden backing to the mirror was also cracked. Inserted between it and the glass were hundreds of pieces of fine yellow paper which came apart in my hands as I picked at them. Someone had used them as a sort of extra backing, perhaps to stop the silver paint from cracking or splitting. As I gently levered off the pieces of paper I noticed some faint marks on them. When I held them up to the light I was able to see a kind of calligraphy, looking like Chinese or Japanese script, the characters spreading at the bottom: dark, inverted flowers, fan-like blossoms pressed between glass and paper.

The Jesuit used to make notes on the people of our village. He came to speak to me three or four times. The last time I saw him he left his notes behind. He was very absent-minded. He used to be in a great hurry, eating and talking all at once. He never sipped his tea as we do, he drank cups of it down in great gulps. I still have the notes he left behind. I can almost read them now. The words are in English. He said that English was the language of science. They are written on very white paper:

Hair: black and straight
Skin Colour: 12
Nose: straight
Eye: 3 (Japanese) (no Mongolian fold)
Ear: protruding, large
Chin: prominent
Skull: peaks at the top of the head

He said he was an amateur anthropologist. I often think about the implications of his study.

I am calling out to Edna. 'Eddie!' I yell. She is not in the house. I wander along the path circling the house. 'Eddie!' The wind is ripping away pieces of the yellow paper I have in my hands. I put the remainder in my pocket. I shall have to protect them by enclosing them in something. Their frailty cannot stand the present. 'Eddie!' I shout. The pines are bending their heads. I enter the dark forest. Splashes of sun enter with me. I part the branches from in front of my face. The cones crunch under my weight.

In the depth of the forest there is a dark figure. I move towards it. The wind has increased. I can hear it screech along the tops of the trees. Under them everything is strangely silent. Needles poke at my eyes. A dark figure in the forest. Two dark figures. The man is wearing a lumberjacket, crouching over Edna. There is peace in her face. Her eyes are closed. The man is grunting. Edna's legs are bare, rocking slightly. I step back into the pines. Edna's cape is on the ground, fluttering. The man rolls over. A wet toadstool glistens. The lovers are bathed in splashes of sunlight. A cone explodes under my feet like a grenade; a bird whirrs into a tree. My hand holding the papers in my pocket sweats.

I know and do not know. A weight settles on my chest. I am no longer free. The papers in my pocket feel like flakes of rust on an old anchor.

'Shan is ill.' Below decks I am in a fever. I gather up the old man's belongings. In the bundle, among his pots and bags of smelly dried fish, I find some paper. It is thin and yellowish. In the hollow bamboo pole to which the bundles are tied I find a pen. It is a bamboo pen with fine pig bristles. I heard it rattle inside the pole when I raised it to remove the bundles. A small bag of coins fell out with it. My head aches and there is a chill in my body.

I mix some of the charcoal from my stove with water. After a while I get the right consistency by drawing off the excess water. I write with this ink on the yellow paper. I do not know why I feel this way. The others do not seem to be ill. My head aches and my hand shakes. I write: 'Time has become the journey.'

It is a matter of recording these thoughts, these events. I write:

'Today the old man was buried at sea. His body was rolled over the gunwale wrapped in canvas and weighed with several links from an old anchor chain. I saw his face before they wrapped him up. It was dark and shrivelled, like the underside of a mushroom. There is a lot of talk on deck about a disease called cholera.'

I am confined to the hold. Below the grating I can hear the sounds of English on deck as I write. Morrison, the master, makes a rare appearance above me. He is worried. His words seem frantic.

'Time has become the journey.' I think that is what is written on one of the sheets of paper. Of course, I cannot read Chinese. Someone called Wah seems to have translated it into English, writing the words under each character down the page, from left to right. I can only just make it out when I hold the sheet up to the light. It looks as though it had been written in pencil or charcoal, and then rubbed out. Perhaps the translator changed his mind, or thought it a wrong translation.

'Eddie?'

'Yes, dear.'

'Does anyone else live around here?'

'Not that I know of. Why?'

'Just wondering.'

'Why do you ask?'

'I thought I saw a person in the forest.'

'Could be a swaggie. We still get them around here.'

'A man in a lumberjacket.'

'I don't know. Have you seen him recently?'

'Yesterday morning.'

'Where?'

'In the forest. Near the boulder.'

'You were near the boulder?'

'I was just walking along there.'

'When were you there?'

'Late morning. Must have been close to midday.'

'Oh.'

'Why? Do you know him?'

'It's probably Fitz.'

'Who's Fitz? What's his name?'

'He's an itinerant worker. Comes to chop wood sometimes. Does some shearing around these parts.'

'I broke the mirror in my room.'

'How did you do that?'

'Don't know. Just fell off its hinges.'

'Can't we glue it back?'

'Don't think so.'

'Never mind, dear.'

The fire cracks and pops. Edna is reading her book. She has not looked up from it.

'Eddie?'

'Yes, Seamus.'

'I found some papers behind the mirror.'

'That's interesting. What are they?'

'Someone's written on them in Chinese or something.'

'Can you read it?'

'How would I be able to read it?'

'Oh, yes. I forgot you can't read Chinese.'

'I can't even speak it.'

'What are you going to do with them?'
'I don't know. It's sort of mysterious.'
'You like to make everything mysterious.'

I have to write for somebody who can understand. Every single Chinaman aboard this ship is illiterate.

'So I shall address you, dear reader, and tell you how the ship made landfall and took on fresh food and water, how we tasted fruit, soft and mushy on our tongues, how the people greeted us with their dark faces and white smiles, how we thought the journey was at an end, and were disappointed at the distance we still had to travel.

'You will probably not even be able to imagine the agony in our hearts, hearing stories of Victoria's golden soil, where men were tripping over nuggets and stubbing their toes on golden boulders. All this coupled with the fact that we had been four months or so at sea, and the journey's end was not in sight. But I have lost all concept of time. For several days now opium has kept my fever in check, my sweat turning glacial, my mind inactive in the frozen wastes of lethargy.

'Two days out after our landfall, the master of the ship called me up on deck. He asked me first, in a mixture of English and Chinese, whether I was still sick. He looked at me carefully from beneath his bushy eyebrows. I replied that since we had taken on food and water I was feeling much better. He asked me how the men were taking the journey. Well enough, I said. He said to tell them that the journey would not be much longer, that we would sight the western coast of the Great South Land in several weeks' time.

'The men were happy with the news. They began to break into the stores they had so carefully reserved for a longer and more difficult period ahead. That night we ate pieces of duck we had preserved in oil, garnished with ginger and mixed with vegetables. We even had some rice wine, and we toasted one another with wishes of gold, luck and health.

'I do not know why I cannot share their happiness. Can it be that there is more joy in departing than in arriving? Would my journey never end?'

Issued at: *Sydney*
Délivré à:
On: 2 *February*
Le:

I have applied for another passport. The man at the passport office gave it to me after a long lecture on the way I had treated my old one. He asked me why I had written all those notes and memos on the pages reserved for visas. He said that some law had been contravened, though he was unable to say which one.

I have suspected all along that it was a compulsion of mine to scribble down my thoughts on any paper that came to hand. The passport was very suitable for this. I carried it around with me all the time. I couldn't do without it; I couldn't let my identity slip out of my hands. It was constantly under threat from the other self. Perhaps it was the watermark on the paper that attracted me, or the way the wavy lines ran through the pages, simulating those on paper money. Perhaps it was the coat-of-arms that seemed to give my thoughts authority.

On the page headed by the words *Remarks/Observations*, I have copied down the comments from my doctor's referral: 'The patient is in good physical health, but is suffering from Hume's syndrome; there is an inability to separate and distinguish the past, present and future. He is also aging prematurely, i.e. his hair is turning white, the skin is beginning to be wrinkled, though blood pressure is normal. He complains of hearing voices and has difficulty pursuing his thoughts.'

Already my photograph does not resemble me. My appearance belies my age, something which may also invest me with authority.

Shan's journals, real and imagined, have merged. Notice how I'm beginning to harness his voice with quotation marks. It fills me with excitement. Not only am I the *author*, the originator, but I am his *progenitor*, having impregnated myself with these fictions.

God, I'm hungry. I've taken a fancy to sweet and sour pork. But I shall not be sidetracked. Let me return to those years at *Twin Groves*.

For about three years Edna taught me all she knew. She prescribed books for me to read, coached me in the skills of biography and translations (things that I have not yet managed to learn). When she saw my developing love of literature she suggested that I sit for the public exams, and that I try for a scholarship. Teaching, she may have thought, would be the cure for my obsessions.

'My dear reader, do not misunderstand my anxiety. My heart did beat faster and my stomach churned with excitement when I first saw the red glimmer on the port rail, the auspicious sunrise bathing the flanks of this land with gold. Surely such warmth and light must promise easy passages ahead, calm seas, a home for troubled spirits?'

I had to go for an interview. They were undecided about whether I was capable of being a teacher. They wanted to give me a reading test. (I discovered later that this was only given to foreigners.)

I took the long train trip to the city. An Aboriginal woman sat opposite me. She was humming and smiling, though she had a bad cough. I noticed that her handkerchief was spotted with blood. The native and the foreigner: there was something of both in us.

In the city I went to a book store and browsed among the shelves to kill time; I bought a copy of *The Trial*, by Franz Kafka. I felt sick, my stomach was knotted and I wanted to vomit. Why would they want to give me a reading test? Would the words jumble themselves before my eyes? Would I spout an incomprehensible stream of Chinese? Would the Pentecostal Spirit descend upon me and make me speak in tongues?

I found the building, which took up the whole block. There were a dozen entrances, but some of these were locked and others were blocked with huge garbage bins and sacks of waste paper. I walked around to the back and the doors there were also locked. Perhaps I had come on the wrong day. A man who appeared to be a kitchen hand pushed a trolley of teacups into a narrow passageway. I asked him where the office was. He looked at me, shook his head, and eased the trolley along the wall. Then he stopped, undid the apron he was wearing, scratched under the armhole of a dirty singlet and pointed to a door on the right.

The creaking lift took me up to the second floor. A receptionist smiled at me and indicated a seat in the waiting-room. Four Asian youths sat along the wall. I smiled at them nervously. One of them was reading half aloud from the *Vogue* he was holding. He was chewing the words in great mouthfuls.

I was called first. The others looked at me as I walked into the room opposite them. Three men were seated behind a table with books and papers in front of them. The man in the middle frowned and pointed to the chair in front of the table. The other two shuffled their papers. Chairs squeaked as they bent forward, and the man in the middle reached for something in his coat. Did he wear a shoulder-holster or was it his braces? He took out a pair of glasses, clicked their handles together, unfolded them, lay them on the table.

'Your name is?'

'Seamus O'Young.'

'That's a strange name for you, isn't it?'

I shook my head. I didn't know. Was this a committee on un-Australian activities?

The other two looked up from their papers. There was an uncomfortable silence. Glasses glinted beneath the white lights.

'What do you intend studying?'

'Well, I'd like to study Chinese.'

There were more frowns.

'I'm sorry, but you have to pick two teaching subjects, and Chinese isn't on the curriculum. What's your next choice?'

I didn't know. I had not been prepared for this. Through the window I caught sight of the giant smokestacks of the power station. This was Auschwitz. Soon, dear Edna, I'll be home.

The chairs creaked. I opened my eyes wide, and must have appeared mentally defective. See, they are blue; I was showing them. I realized then that when I applied for a scholarship the local authorities had mistaken me for a Chinaman.

'You like languages?' the man in the middle continued.

'I guess ... not particularly.'

'How about French? We're very short of French teachers.'

'Well ...'

'We'll put down French and History. Please read from that book in front of you.

The book was open on page 160. The heading at the top of the page said, *'The Yellow Race'*. I began to read. I trilled my r's, arched my a's, made the p's sound like b's. I sounded like the Queen.

'Before the discovery of gold there were relatively few of the Celestials in Australia. However, in the fifties the yellow tide threatened to engulf the country. The white race was partially to blame for spreading rumours in Chinese ports that fortunes could be made here ...'

'Thank you. That will be all for now.'

I went out. Four pairs of eyes along the wall glanced at me nervously.

Four weeks after I had passed my written examinations, they sent me a letter telling me I had gained the scholarship.

'The shoreline is never-ending. Yesterday I saw huge cliffs battered by waves. Our ship sailed fairly close in several times and I thought we would be dashed on to the great walls. As we made one run in I almost wished that we would. I was anxious to be physically a part of this country. I felt that those walls were external and internal to myself; external because they would never be breached from the sea; internal because I imagine that I am already on the other side, standing on the cliff, looking out to sea, anxious not to be breached, I felt both foreign and native. Perhaps I was eager not to be threatened by the new.

'I thought of my father, sitting at home, listening for the sound of petals dropping onto the stone floor.'

Shan. I have discovered something in the way you wrote your name. You wrote it like a mountain rearing up from the page; three pennants signalling your daring. Isn't it a too-vigorous demonstration of your self? Are you afraid of being deprived of your identity?

So you are discovering a new land, and yourself as well,

modifying your views, readjusting your stance. How much
of your foreignness will you retain, how much will you lose?
Hasn't your journey then been in effect a translation of yourself
and a transition for me? (You have begun to learn English, and
I Chinese.) Shall we come to know each other through such
adjustments?

'A hundred petals about to fall at once. That was how the faces of the men looked when they were told of the poll-tax they
would have to pay if we landed in Victoria. Morrison strode up
and down the deck explaining the situation to me.

'"Chinese immigrants have to pay £10 each for landing. But
we will get round the problem. We will land at Guichen Bay.
From there it's only a short walk to the gold. You fellows will be
rich men. Now that'll be worth it, won't it? None of you can pay
the tax, and they'll want it from me. Now you tell them not to
worry."

'His voice sounded far away. It seemed that he had prepared
a speech and had committed it to memory. I struggled with the
formality of it, and translated it to the men. Their faces showed
a mixture of incomprehension and disbelief. They looked like
gamblers who had been cheated.

'The ship swung on a starboard tack. It was a fine, warm and
cloudless day. The shore loomed ominously. We made a long
reach and then came about, the canvas luffing and then strain-
ing with loud snaps. There was a steady muttering, and then
there was a sound like a sifting of dirt, a sigh which did not come
from the men who were staring anxiously at the shore. The ship
slowed and listed. Suddenly there was a terrible thumping and
cracking. The sails expelled the air like pierced balloons. There
was a lot of shouting. Water began to fill the hold. Wood began
to part. I rushed like the others to collect my belongings. We
made rafts from the tea-chests that we hauled on deck.

'It was the second day of February 1857, and there wasn't a cloud in the sky.'

3 THE PROMISING LAND

Boulogne-sur-Mer

Damned near froze my ass off. That is the sort of line they use in American novels. I had never seen beaches covered in snow. At the hovercraft station they made us wait two hours and then transferred us in buses, everyone swearing, to the car ferry.

I walk down the long concrete ramp. A Japanese woman in front of me is loaded with five bags of various dimensions,— rice cooker and tea kettle falling out of one—and a suitcase too large for her that she is dragging down the ramp, ripping out the bottom. Perhaps I will help her, and she will smile at me out of a pure and fresh face and we will say nothing to each other all the way down; and I will think of all the border crossings we will do separately, in our own fashion, she smiling and walking straight through, I with a dark scowl being searched, cold fingers running down my legs. No one will know of the bomb she will drag through several countries in that suitcase, until it is too late. So, with that possibility in mind, I do not help her.

We had a rough passage of it. The Channel disgorged its dirtiest bile, the sea boiling and chafing relentlessly, tossing the ferry in its freezing grey slops, the white caps slurring misty spindrift from crest to crest, the waves meeting the ship head on, drumming out hasty consonants and dispelling the steady rhythm of its engines. It was then that I began to think of Shan and wondered why I had not thought about him these last four years, he who had placed so much trust in his reader, such trust as to burden me with the responsibility for his very existence.

I had let him down. I knew that. Yet it was impossible for me to do otherwise. I reminded myself that Shan had left great yawning gaps in his writing. I had been at a loss in trying to piece it together. Were the fragments I had discovered behind the mirror all that remained of Shan's journal? Was his life erased for ever?

You see how I still cannot hear his voice. Shan, what was your fate in that land? Why did you become silent as I have been for the last four years? Perhaps if I explain my silence you will somehow come to me again from across the chasm of time.

I have been living in the worlds of books and languages. They have imprisoned and confused me. Time; reality; structure. The bars of my cell. The inner life composed entirely of words was proving agonizing. Is this the price one has to pay to flesh out another existence? I began to wonder if Shan were my reason for being. Was he creating me out of this silence, so that, deprived of his voice, I could discover my own?

For three years I had learnt how to give my life direction, while living on my meagre allowance which was augmented from time to time by Edna's generosity. For three years I studied, taking the subjects set out for me as well as attending night classes to learn the language that was most essential for me. For three years I lived in the city, watching the seasons change and change again; watching the storms lash the buildings and the sea turn wild; baking in the heat on depressing afternoons when the trucks unleashed their fumes into the still air; hearing men's shouts and neighbours' quarrels floating over fences, listening to the steady drone of suburbia.

It was a shock for me when I returned to the farmhouse to see the big pines cut down, the house standing bare and white in the sunlight, the wood stacked neatly by the door. It was a shock, after knocking on the door, to have it opened by a swarthy, unshaven man in a green lumberjacket, Edna peering out at me from behind him short-sightedly. And then there was her smile, her embarrassment at introducing me to Fitzpatrick.

'Fitz is staying with us now,' she had said, smiling again; and I thought of the 'us', and my mind went back to another night years ago.

I did not stay. Fitzpatrick turned out to be nice enough, not gruff as I had imagined him to be. He said little and kept to himself that afternoon, brooding over his whisky, offering one or two unexpected remarks about socialism. When I left that night, without accepting their entreaties to stay, I felt empty. As I drove along the dirt track leading away from the house, my headlights mesmerizing several rabbits, I thought how this emptiness within me was extended by the environment: when once I would have sought sanctuary in it, now my mind was filled with words rattling in its silence. There was a struggle between words and the land. How the battle raged in my mind!

It was perhaps for this reason that I applied for my first teaching post in a land whose mind was concerned with being and nothingness, whose language bounded one's existence.

They sent me to a ghetto near Paris surrounded by cemeteries, and for a year I studied the meaning of solitude, holed up in a room watching the sleet and snow cake the dried sausages I hung outside my window. For a year I experienced the life of the mind, hasheesh, anarchy and loud foreign language classes. For a year I wandered down corridors in a large concrete school looking for my noisy pupils, herding them into ordered rows of berets, scarfs and rain-flecked woollens. For a year I experienced the constant humming of the electric lights, the walk to the early morning classes through the black streets, the rich smell of dark tobacco. I tagged along on the ends of loud jokes at the lunch table, was dragged into the warm fug of brasseries and laughed alongside bottles of wine, apprehension building as the hour of classes approached. For a year I read, talked, learnt to curl my tongue around the language.

Not once did I feel any desolation or the need to retreat to that oasis of my Sahara, not once did I look through a hole at the world. I was out in the open, seeing everything. It was strange then, that I should yearn for that desert, as though there could be something there left unfinished, something that gave me power over myself.

Was it irresponsibility then, or a kind of anarchy, that inspired me to walk out of that school one dark winter morning and catch the train to the channel port? One thing led to another. I was not able to control my actions, I'm sure of that.

The customs officer looked at me for a long time as he held my passport. In the next queue a black girl shouted and screamed. He turned his head and said something to me. Before I could correct him, he waved me through. ABC stands for Australian-born Chinese, I should have said. The screaming intensified. Entering countries, like entering life itself, is a painful thing.

I am in the train going up to London. I have the compartment all to myself, though there was a huge crowd at the station. People were banked up like bottles at the end of a production line.

The train is moving very slowly. Suddenly the door of my compartment is flung open, and a large woman enters. She has dark hair. I see the back of her head first, as she backs into the compartment with two large suitcases propping the door open. Under her arms are wedged a couple of large picture frames. She is wearing a black cape, which is getting in her way. I offer to help her. She turns round. Her face is not pretty, but it is a striking one. Her eyebrows are painted heavily, her cheeks rouged, her lips red and wide, blooming like a large rose with teeth as she smiled. She looks almost like a clown.

'Thank you,' she says, her breath hot on my neck and smelling of garlic as I stoop to pick up her suitcases. We stumble over each other. We are finally in our seats.

'My name is Fatima,' she says, offering her small hand, which is damp and cold. With her other hand she unbuttons her cape. Large breasts heave in time to her breathing.

'Seamus O'Young.'

'You're Australian.'

'How would you know that?'

'I can tell immediately from your accent.'

'You must be one too then.'

'Sydney.'

'Fascinating.'

'Sydney?'

'No. That we're here together.'

'Not really. There are Aussies everywhere.'

'No, I mean it's a strange name, Fatima.'

'My mother was Portuguese. It's really Fatiminha, but that's a mouthful. I'm a painter.'

'Oh?'

'Others say artist, but I prefer painter. It's more exact.' The train punches through a snow-storm. I am enchanted by Fatima. Slowly she weaves her spell over me. It is the way she talks, the movement of her eyes and mouth, the gestures she uses. Her eyes are a deep green, and they hold mine with a steadiness that drowns my gaze. There is a long silence. She offers me chocolate. Suddenly she speaks:

'I would love to paint you.'

It was a line that disappointed me. One of the reasons I have never been attracted to young artists is that their language is always a disappointment.

'I would not like to be painted—or photographed, for that matter.'

'Why? Are you afraid of yourself?'

'On the contrary. I just hate to be seen.'

'That's a pity.'

'I've never thought of it as a pity.'

'I think you should be seen.'

'Why, and by whom?'

'By everyone of course. A blue-eyed white-haired Chinaman is an anomaly. Perhaps you're an albino ... which makes it even more interesting.'

'I'm aging prematurely. The doctors can't make it out. That accounts for the white hair.'

'Look, don't get me wrong. I wasn't referring ...'

'That's OK.'

I liked the way she spoke, regardless of what she said.

'What I mean is that it's not the subject in painting that should be studied, but the process or references of which the subject is a part. For instance, in your case, what would the painting of you be saying about time, or about race, or memory?'

In a way Fatima reminded me of Edna. There was a willingness to plunge straight into theory in an attempt to distance herself from embarrassing intimacy. All was possible within theory. Great emotions could have been housed in those dispassionate words.

'A body describes itself by its lines of tension,' she went on, 'by its wanting to become invisible, not exhibitory. It should never be conscious that it is being seen: that is its attraction.'

Something in the pocket of my overcoat was making me uncomfortable. I stood up and took off the coat. In one pocket I found a block of Toblerone. I don't know why they make it such an awkward shape. I broke it in half and offered the triangles of chocolate to her. She refused it.

'Too much weight,' she said.

The train seemed to be slowing.

'Furthermore the painter shouldn't even have the intention that the painting should be seen. That is its real value, don't you think so?'

She gave a European tilt to the question. I wondered how long she had lived in Europe. Without waiting for my reply she went on:

'Wanting to be invisible, you are nevertheless seen and noticed. All the time. You are part of the process of a kind of unintentional documentation; you are recorded in people's minds, and in the course of time (almost instantly in some cases) you are forgotten and you become invisible again. Art too, draws on memory, though people have tried to mystify the process by calling it the artist's unconscious. A painter may dredge up a face from memory and in the course of painting it endow it with her style, with her personality, so the process is finally a celebration, an affirmation of the subject's life. Isn't this what you do with others? Isn't your memory of them a continuation of their lives?'

'Yes, that's quite obvious, but ...'

'But what? Art is the obvious. It's a record of the way people think, feel, act. There are only two subjects: life and death. Now take the photograph. That is a record of death. Time, that time in the photo, stands still. The people in it die. A painting springs from an abstraction. The painter's mental references are still there; fresh, undiminished.'

She went on. She was quite animated now, speaking with her hands. Perhaps she was irritated by my lack of response. I was fascinated with the movement of her mouth, the expression on her face, her eyes, her breasts under the red dress, the way she pulled at the elastic around her sleeves, her dainty feet like tiny blossoms encased in small, high-heeled slippers.

I had been thinking so much of all this that I did not realize she had stopped speaking. Suddenly she said 'Excuse me', and moved unsteadily out of her seat to the door. She walked quickly and disappeared up the corridor. There was a faint whiff of Lanvin perfume and garlic in the compartment.

Her words stirred my imagination. I thought of Shan, tried to visualize his face. Suddenly I was interrupted by a middle-aged man bumping his way with a suitcase into the compartment. He sat down, breathing heavily in his tweed overcoat. He smiled at me. He had a kind face that seemed overcome by sadness, perhaps because of the drooping eyelids, the heavy, bent nose and bushy eyebrows. I thought of Fatima's words.

The train had stopped. The man looked gloomily out the window at a laundry van bogged in a snowdrift, at the mounds of exhaust fumes, at the spinning wheels. He rested his elbow on the windowsill and stroked with a long finger at the whitish hair (stained nicotine-yellow at the edges) near his temple. I offered him some of my chocolate.

'No, thank you very much indeed.' He smiled. So he was French. He offered me a hand. I shook it. It was dry, warm and soft.

'Seamus O'Young,' I said.

'Barthes, Roland.'

When the train started again, he stood up, apologized and said that he was in the wrong compartment. Perhaps he had been looking for solitude. I kept the door from sliding against him.

I put on my overcoat. I am moving up the corridor to the buffet. Outside the windows there is a white world. Black-faced sheep stare at the train from holes in the snow. I feel slightly dizzy. My stomach is purring with hunger. At the end of the corridor I come to the toilet. The little dial says that it is not occupied. I push open the small door.

Fatima is sitting there, her dress up around her large thighs, her hands and arms cradling the folds of her red dress, her stockings rolled down to her ankles. She looks at me smiling. I close the door quickly and try to bolt it from the outside, pushing at the letters on the dial with my penknife. The jolting train makes it impossible. All I do is scratch the dial and push open the door again. I hurry to the buffet. The train skates through a frozen town.

The buffet was too crowded. I returned to my compartment, my hands in my overcoat pockets, steadying myself with my elbows. My hand felt a thick envelope, a letter I had picked up from my box before leaving the school. I opened it slowly and took out a bundle of yellow papers bound with a rubber band. I knew what they were immediately.

> My dear Seamus,
> I thought you would want to have these. Fitz and I were cleaning out the spare room the other day and we found them in between the drawers in the old lowboy. We salvaged as much as we could, though the mice got to a lot of it. There were several sheets behind the big mirror on the door as well. Someone has used them for backing and they are stained and tend to break up in your hands ... hope you find something interesting in them.
> Are you keeping warm? We heard about the terrible weather in Europe ...

I looked at the pieces of yellow paper. Shan's unmistakable writing. I folded them carefully and put them back in the envelope. Several flakes of yellow paper remained on my fingers.

Fatima returned smiling. 'Here,' she said, 'I got you a sandwich. I knew you wouldn't want to go to the buffet. It's terribly crowded there.'

She sat down next to me and handed me a sandwich wrapped in plastic.

He came ashore soaked, stinking of seaweed, exhausted and stung by jellyfish, clinging to a tea chest. The sweetish perfume of tea was in his hair as he rested on the beach below the town called Robe, an ironic mantle for his shivering bones.

He staggered along with the others. They must have looked like strange creatures from the sea, clutching their meagre belongings, trailing great lengths of kelp behind them, dragging poles or sacks filled with pots which they gathered from the water's edge. All these moon-faced men with pigtails, stepping ashore from another age. The local inhabitants came in droves and stood along the edge of the dunes gaping at them.

For a long time the men stood or squatted in the sand, the wind drying their clothes. No one had drowned. Some swam ashore as he did, half paddling, half floating for three miles. Others were picked up by local fishing-boats, the owners of which charged exorbitant prices for those who could not swim.

It had been a long day. He shivered. The sick afternoon light penetrated his head, and it seemed like a presentiment of death, the blinding harshness of it mixed with the cold end of the day. The land smelt of eucalyptus, like the anointing oil his countrymen used for the sick, balms for the dying; it smelt of the dusty eeriness of primitive history. The salt clung to his face. He began to erect a tent in the scrub not far from the beach. The tall Shanghainese and two others followed him and pooled their resources. They fixed their bamboo poles into the ground and stretched a sheet of canvas sail over them. After a meal of cooked rice and some vegetables they managed to buy from a local farmer, they settled down for the evening.

It was good to be on dry land, Shan thought to himself, even though the land rolled and pitched like a gigantic ship. Sitting by the light of the fire, the four men stared up at the trees and the clear night sky. Around them other fires flickered from encampments in the hollow. They did not speak much. They tried to imagine the distance they still had to travel. It was difficult to grasp the idea that they had four or five hundred miles to walk.

> *'In this rough hollow*
> *protected by slivers*
> *of moonlit rock*
> *not far from pounding surf*
> *I wrap myself in earth*
> *fearful still of ghosts.*
> *In the hiatus between*
> *each roar*
> *I listen for my sadness*
> *sighing before*
> *each curling wave's*
> *unharnessed.'*

Morning. Shan's poem flutters beside the warm coals. A breeze stirs the men farther up the gully. Fires are kindled, the smoke drifting lazily between the hills, the sound of cracking wood sharp as ice breaking in a morning thaw. Shan hears the thumping of a dozen hatchets in soft, decaying wood. Next to the tent, the Shanghainese jumps on a dead branch.

On the beach men are gathering driftwood. At the far end a dark figure is approaching. It makes its way along the dunes, stepping carefully over driftwood. It is coming towards the men, who stop gathering the wood and begin to form into groups, pointing at the figure. Soon they can see him quite clearly. It is a Chinese man, dressed in Western clothes. He wears a long tail coat and trousers tucked into shiny, knee-length boots, rubbing them on the backs of his trousers each time he sinks into the sand. He wears a black bowler hat and carries a carpet-bag. The men are wary of this strange figure which seemed to have materialized out of the sand-dunes. The tails of his coat drag in the sand each time he steps into troughs in the beach. The man is puffing; he is not a young man. When he removes his hat to wipe the perspiration from his forehead, they can see his bald and greying head.

'Good morning,' says he to the men who are staring at him. He smiles. 'My name is Big Wah. I'm known here as Wally. I've just come back from the goldfields.' As he speaks he waggles his stubby fingers. He is quite clearly unaccustomed to wearing the huge gold rings encrusting them.

'I have had some good fortune,' he continues, noticing that the faces of the men show a new respect.

'Where are the old men?' he asks self-importantly.

The men point up at the hillside. Shouts ring out. Several old men appear from their tents like moles, blinking in the sunlight. Despite their ragged appearance, they arrange themselves in a circle with great formality, and then sit down on logs around a pit filled with charred wood and glowing embers. They are prepared to receive their visitor. Wah approaches and remains standing until an old man motions him to sit. The other men crowd around. Wah is given a mug filled with hot tea. After several sips of tea he is asked by the old man to speak.

'I have come from Ballarat,' he begins. 'As you see, I have had some good luck. For years I hadn't found more than a speck, then I came across a lump of gold just like that, after three or four prods with my shovel. Now I am going to buy some property here, settle down. Chinaman's nugget they called it ... a lump the size of your fist.'

The men looked at the rings, the gold reflected in their eyes. Wah continued, talking into his mug of tea: 'There's still gold. They're finding it here and there. But it's not easy.' The men smile. Nothing has been easy. 'Yes, a farm, that's what I'm after. I'll grow vegetables. I'll build a large house, carve it out of a forest ...' Wah has forgotten himself. The old men are uneasy.

'But why have you come here?' they ask him.

Wah takes another sip. His face loses its smile. Something is unhinged when he tries to speak again. His mouth opens and shuts weakly.

'There is a lot of resentment against us Chinese,' he says. 'When I first arrived there were ugly incidents. People were hurt. It's important to abide by the rules. But there is a lot of malice. The white man doesn't like success unless it is his own. Get your gold and get out ... that's what I say. I've got nothing to go back to, but you've got your wives, your families. Don't be greedy.'

The old men nod. There is wisdom in this. Wah takes on the advisory role of a benevolent elder.

'There is a licence of £1 a month for digging. Some people haven't been getting this licence. The Chinese have been blamed. There is talk among the whites of forming an anti-Chinese league. This means that we could all be chased out and our gold confiscated. You'll agree that that would be the end for some of us. You'll never get home and you'll becomes slaves.'

There is a lot of muttering from the men. One old man holds up his hand for silence. It is a long time before he speaks:

'What else, Wah, have you come to tell us?' he asks.

'Your group should draw up a set of rules. For one thing, thieving should be strictly forbidden. In our camp thieves were dealt ten strokes of the cane. If you keep your own house in order, it will be difficult for the white devils to find fault. They have a sense of justice, but it has got to be on their terms. Old customs and "fair-play" sometimes clash. It is a matter of attitude, which, being part of human nature, shifts and turns like the tide. Secondly, they have a saying: "Cleanliness is next to Godliness."'

The men burst out laughing.

'Oh, you may laugh,' Wah continues, 'but you will very quickly be accused of dirtying the water or spreading disease. Any of these excuses will be used for driving you from the fields.' He pauses, wipes his mouth with an immaculately white handkerchief. 'Thirdly you must not have bare heads. Or bare feet.

Dress like the white man. Do not wear your Chinese trousers. See how I am dressed.'

He stands up, displays his coat, his boots. He pirouettes, loses his balance, sits down clumsily.

'We have nothing to buy clothes with,' the old man says to him. Wah looks down at his boots. He is ashamed. He has been arrogant to his own people. A piece of yellow paper flutters near his boots. He scuffs at it. He sees several more jammed between the log and the ground. Unconsciously he picks them up, stuffs them in his pocket. After so many years of fossicking, it has become second nature to him: anything yellow, golden vaguely valuable. The old man rises.

'Thank you for your advice,' he says, placing a hand on Wah's padded shoulder. 'I'm glad you have found your fortune. You are a very lucky man. Your visit has been beneficial for all of us. I'm sure you have brought us some of your luck.'

The men disperse. Wah throws the rest of his tea in the fire, stands up, picks up his bag and walks back to the beach.

As he passes the last tent he sees a man leaning up against a tree. The man motions him to stop. 'I hope you are successful with your farm,' the man says. Wah nods. 'By the way,' the man continues, 'what do they call us, these white devils?'

'Two things,' Wah shouts, resuming his way without turning round. 'From now on you are either a Celestial or simply "John Chinaman".'

Shan thinks about this for a long while. The naming of names has been bothering him.

Wah was also thinking of names. His farm will have a nice Chinese name. He could not have known that a century later it would bear the name *Twin Groves*.

'We stayed two days at Robe, bartering and buying supplies for our long march ahead. We found the local population friendly

and helpful. They seemed to have acquired a taste for our preserved ginger, and we found that we could use this for bartering. Others expressed a keen interest in our opium for "medic-
inal purposes". As yet we had not found a pilot who could take
us to Ballarat. Most of the locals were reluctant to venture that
distance, leading a hundred Celestials on a pilgrimage to the
Gold Mountain.

'I have three companions. The tall Shanghainese, whose
name is Tzu, is a great optimist and a good worker. Each day
he does the hard work of chopping wood and carrying water.
The other two are less efficient. Wang, a wily-looking northern-
er with a pockmarked face, favours opium too much. He talks
too much of gambling and smuggling. Ah Pan, the youngest
member of our party, is a sweet-faced boy who dreams a good
deal and is totally useless in practical matters, though he tries
hard. But he does keep up our spirits with his constant singing,
humming the familiar village songs from our native province.

'The four of us were able to buy several tin dishes, a "pud-
dling tub", a pick, shovel and some stout boots. The boots hurt
my feet a lot at first, but I remembered Wah's words, and persevered with them, raising large blisters on the sides of my toes.

'A man finally offered to lead us to Ballarat, a fair-haired
Irishman who exacted what he called a "small" fee from us.
Our whole company of a hundred men managed to raise £50
between us.

'"Dere tough roads between here and the gold," the Irishman said. "Yer won't be sorry yer got me ter take yer dere
meself." He had a habit of squinting when he spoke, and none
of us trusted him. "Dere's dem Vandemonians on de roads dese
days. Tousands of criminal men bent on robbin' poor devils like
yerselves."

'Sure enough, two days out from Robe he disappeared like a
ghost into thin air.'

I married Fatima back in Sydney in a grey registry office lined with filing cabinets smelling of disinfectant. It was a cloudless day. Fatima was crying either with joy or with anguish. She looked like a large blue hydrangea sprinkled with droplets of dew. Her mascara was blue, her lipstick blue, her hair dyed blue.

'I am so nervous,' she said, trembling in a thin blue dress. Her tight, blue high-heeled shoes threatened to snap.

'Fatima Fernanda,' intoned the celebrant, 'do you take this man ...?'

So it was done. She signed the certificate: Fatima Fernanda Feingold.

Suddenly it began to rain. It had been a fine, cloudless day. The sky was blue. 'A monkey's wedding,' Fatima said. Edna used to say that on days like this one had to take 'an extra suck on the monkey', meaning, in her case, another bottle of brandy before lunch. There was a card from her, with a cheque pinned to it. At the back of the card, fixed with a paperclip, was a bundle of yellow papers.

They jog-trotted along the dirt roads, swinging their loads from one shoulder to the other as they avoided the ruts and holes. Their bundles went up and down to the rhythm of their jog, bending and flexing the bamboo poles. As they approached each town the locals turned out to gape at this rag-tag army of blue-shirted, moon-faced Celestials.

He was unaccustomed to their stares. He was too self-conscious. He thought they were singling him out. He wanted to merge into the sea of moon faces. In that tide there was anonymity, salvation.

He was wrong, of course. He was not being singled out. He wondered about the others. Perhaps their ignorance protected them from self-consciousness and over-sensitivity.

'Again I begin to set myself apart. I am beginning to doubt my motives for coming here. Did I really come for adventure and to discover gold?

Ah Pan struggles with his load ahead of me, singing still, grunting in the heat of the day, the flies accompanying his song with their insistent harmonies. My survival is with these, my people. Yet it pains me to speak to them, so apart am I from their beliefs. I share all with them but my thoughts. These I reserve for you, dear reader!'

In those first months of my marriage to Fatima I had a fairly clear picture of Shan struggling towards Ballarat in the heat of the day. It was as though his manuscript were no longer simply a palimpsest of censored thoughts but a reel of film, each character framed and appearing to me so vividly that I was able to visualize the private and secret meditations behind each stroke of the calligraphy. It was a skill that I owed to Fatima. It was she who taught me many things about seeing of which I was totally unconscious before. Her gift to me was to clear a path that enabled me to find out something about myself.

Fatima and I never really discovered each other sexually. We were always seeking ways of conjoining our minds but never our bodies. This was probably the reason for our marriage. Our arrangement was rational, seemingly dispassionate. I was enticed by the intangible aspects of Fatima's body, by gestures, movement; but could not bring myself to physical expressions of love. Fatima, for her part, seemed even repelled by any sexual caressing, though this, she always hastened to imply, did not rule out sexual love.

At first it seemed that such a relationship was not possible, but gradually I was able to understand that immense gratification was possible only through absences. The absence of touch, the absence of proximity, the absence of any possibility of sexual contact, was what created Fatima's wholeness for me. It was in this abnegation that I saw her entirely.

It probably happened by accident. I must have been peering through a gap in the wall, or through a crack in the door, when I saw her lying naked on the bed, arranging her body in different positions: propping herself up on her elbows and knees so that her pendulous breasts grazed the silken bedsheets, or posing before the mirror, her hand lightly obscuring the dark fork in her thighs.

I did not know whether she was aware of my watching. It was then that the pieces fell into place. I remembered her saying that a body should not be conscious that it was being seen; that there should not even be the intention of seeing. It was this unintentional documentation, this unplanned voyeurism, that described our sexual relationship; the process of casual, carnal witnessing. This, then, was her gift to me. All of a sudden I realized that whereas previously what I saw filled me with an inexplicable power and control, now it was only in total self-control and abnegation that I could see clearly. Marriage to Fatima was my licence for this conscious rendering of vicarious sexuality. It was legalized voyeurism. Battle-lines were drawn up between chastity and masturbation. The concept in its initial form wasn't new, for priests in confessionals have been practising this dialectic for centuries. It was said to have led to enlightenment if chastity prevailed. The other way led to blindness.

Clancy came out of his mud-brick cottage in the early morning ... overflowed from it, hitching up his trousers and looking up at the low roof. A large black and white bird was picking at something among the neat squares of turf. It stooped, hopped back and fluttered its wings. It kept one beady eye from its cocked head on the man below. Clancy picked up a rock from the ground. Slowly he aimed and then let fly, his arm arching in a practised, almost horizontal swing.

'Garn, yer bastid,' he said, smiling as the rock whistled an inch from the bird's tail when it flew off heavily with a great flapping of its wings.

At the small window of the hut a rare sight appeared in the form of a golden braid of hair draped over a white dressing-gown.

'Bully!' A soft voice, sweet as the dew, emerged from the narrow casement, teasing; and there was something melodious in those two syllables alone.

Clancy smiled his broad smile, revealing white, gapped teeth. He hitched up his trousers again and strode to the outhouse, a small bark-walled cubicle containing two small logs placed over a hole in the ground. As he sat on the logs, his trousers awkwardly around his boots, he thought about how good he was feeling. He hadn't felt so good in years. He wondered why.

Ever since the Eureka incident three years ago he had been in a terrible depression. He ran the events over in his mind again. His heart beat faster as he repeated the oath he had sworn under that beautiful flag on that last Thursday in November: 'We swear by the Southern Cross to stand truly by each other, and fight to defend our rights and liberties.'

Then his tongue soured again, and he asked himself what did it mean now, to speak of 'rights' and of 'liberties?' A furry caterpillar crawled slowly across the bark wall in front of his eyes. Voices were again roaring in his ears, voices that united nations of men, soon to dissolve into words devoid of meaning, the flag a tower of Babel. Then the voices faded and he heard the screaming of the wounded and the dying, being pierced again and again by bayonets. It was horrifying, senseless. There was no organization, no training, no understanding of the realities. A few idealistic men like himself cowered in their tents while their comrades screamed in their shepherd's holes, exposed to the fire and steel of Her Majesty's forces. He clapped his hands over his ears. The shouting intensified. The caterpillar moved with agonizingly slow undulations towards a chink in the wall. A fetid stench like that of rotten cabbages rose from the hole beneath his pale haunches.

Clancy forgot his happiness. He knew he was totally incapable of action and this understanding of himself tortured him, the foundations of his idealism crumbling into a pit of depression. He yearned for the kind of feeling that inspired mobs. The voices pierced his eardrums. He looked through the chink in the bark wall.

He wasn't dreaming. The voices came from behind the trees, from the road that wound past his hut towards Ballarat. He saw a long blue snake made up of men in large straw hats. They talked as they jogged along the road, their voices making a sound like a hundred violins being tuned. The caterpillar plugged up the hole. The voices trailed towards him.

'More bloody Celestials,' he grunted.

> *'Ching chong Chinaman*
> *sitting on a log*
> *eating the guts*
> *out of Tommy frog.'*

I was a victim and a cannibal. Persecution and grandeur.

Ignorance and mysticism. Intimidation and respectful uncertainty. When I was at school I was both victim and cannibal. I was respected for my mystical barbarism; I was taunted for being inferior as such. I was a wild animal in a cage, gazed at, prodded. My inscrutability rapidly became demystified.

One afternoon I found myself in the science lab. Everyone had gone home. In the next room I could hear the cleaners talking, putting up the chairs, lighting their cigarettes. They had forgotten to lock the lab. I found the frog we were using in biology. The teacher had left it in the sink. I ate it. It tasted like seaweed and a little like caviar and chicken. It left an aftertaste like the slime from a pond.

Now as I begin my teaching in Australia, I hear the same sing-song voices I used to hear in the boys' home, along the corridors. In the exercise book belonging to my prize pupil I note the remark written beneath a previous essay: 'O'Young is a dirty slant-eye.'

The woman also saw them coming. She stood at the window, unmoving, a Pre-Raphaelite woman, the first rays of the sun falling on to her hair and making it sparkle as though flecks of gold dust had been sprinkled through it. Her lips were pale and trembled slightly. She was about to call out to Clancy, but changed her mind. She went quickly to the bedroom, the only other room in the hut, changed into her long dress, donned a black cape and straw bonnet, and walked out the back door to the top of the little hill perforated with holes from recent digging.

She watched the figures approaching. When they reached the section of road that was just below the rise their voices grew silent. The old men, the leaders of the procession, smiled up at her from under their straw hats. She noticed that their faces were gnarled and weather-beaten. She smiled back. The old men stopped. The procession closed like a concertina, the line shunting and folding to a stop. A young man came forward.

'Is Ballarat this way?' he asked, pronouncing each syllable carefully, pointing at the road ahead of him. The young woman nodded.

'Not far now,' she said. She was conscious of the way she kept the information to just three words, as though any elaboration would not be understood. She was struck by the man's smooth-skinned good looks, his flashing white teeth as he smiled at her.

Suddenly she heard a noise behind her, and as she turned she saw Clancy struggling up the hill, tugging at his trousers.

'What do they want?' he shouted to her.

'The way to Ballarat,' she said softly, the shock of his gruffness not having an immediate effect. He reached the top of the rise panting, tying the rope round the top of his trousers.

'Garn, yer bastids!' he yelled suddenly, his voice sounding like a crow's. 'No gold!' he shouted at them. 'No gold! Go back to where you came from.' He waved his arms at them. The Chinamen smiled at him uncomprehendingly. He jumped up and down waving his fist. 'Bloody parasites!'

The young man returned to his position in the queue. They shouldered their bundles and the procession moved off, the men silent, their smiles vanishing with each step they took. Clancy pushed the young woman roughly towards the hut.

Fatima has succeeded beyond her wildest dreams. In only a few years she has become a noted art dealer, and owns a little gallery in the exclusive part of the city. All day she nibbles cakes, sips sherries and hangs paintings. Her life is already beginning to separate itself from mine.

I do not move in her circle of friends; I have difficulty understanding their language. I prefer to look at their paintings, and find that their imaginary worlds are similar to mine. Their minds are just as disordered, self-involved, obsessed. But, as with all mental cases, there is no possibility of communication between us.

I recognize what they are doing, the better ones, that is. Sometimes there is a movement of souls between us ... a grunting acknowledgment, the sound of the sipping of drinks, the infinite stare into space. And that is all there is. Others, I am sure, only tolerate me because I am Fatima's husband.

In the staff wash-room I look in the mirror above the small white sinks. I see lines along my face, lines intersecting and branching off at right angles so that the skin is divided neatly into quadrilaterals. It is a face like a road map; like W.H. Auden's. When I smile the lines increase. My hair is greying. I am aging prematurely.

A strong westerly wind is blowing, and through the window I see the flurries of dust it sends into the quadrangle and along the covered walkways. Children's heads line the sills of a classroom. I wonder what I am doing here.

The lined face stares back at me. I place my hand in the pocket of my coat. There is a piece of paper there, folded neatly in two. It is a resignation form that I have been carrying around with me for several days.

I place the form in my other pocket, where it is more comfortable, and I walk to the headmaster's office.

I make a resolution as the dust blows into my eyes. Tomorrow I will begin fasting to get back my strength.

'What do you say is wrong with you?'

'I have Thalassaemia.'

'What?'

'It's a blood disorder. Like anaemia. It's a hereditary thing, peculiar to people from the Mediterranean region. Also China, Indonesia and India. It's from the Greek word "thalassa" meaning "sea". It's symptoms are Mongolism, enlarged spleen, folded eyelids, indented bridge of the nose. It can be fatal.'

'I see.'

A gleam came into the headmaster's eyes. He had been proved correct. These Orientals were disease carriers.

'It's highly contagious.' This was untrue.

'Oh.'

He is startled, moves back in his chair. But then he is a head-master and not a doctor.

'Transmitted to people in close proximity ...'

'Well, all the best to you. Just leave your form over there. Thank you.' He is anxious not to prolong the interview. 'Goodbye.'

I walk from his office, through the playground, out the gates. I feel a hundred years old. It is the beginning of my solitude.

Dr Z: What are his daily habits?

Fatima: He gets up early, boils enough jasmine tea to fill a thermos-flask and locks himself in his room.

Dr Z: Does he stay there all day?

F: I don't know, because I leave at nine and I'm not home until six in the evening. His door is still locked when I get home.

Dr Z: Have you ever tried to find out what he does in his room?

F: I looked through the keyhole once—when he left the key out of it. He just sat at his desk. He seemed to be meditating.

Dr Z: Meditating?

F: Yes. He was rocking backwards and forwards, reciting some gibberish. Now and again he would hum.

Dr Z: Does he come out to eat? Is there any evidence of food or plates left in the kitchen?

F: Oh, no. He says that he is a monk and that he is on a perpetual fast. Sometimes I've seen an apple core in the bin. But that's all.

Dr Z: Is there anything in his room to indicate what he is meditating on?

F: I got in there early one morning and I noticed a pile of yellowish papers on his desk. He must have been in the process of covering them in plastic. I remember he ordered a whole roll of the stuff one day.

Dr Z: I see. What were these papers like?

F: They were yellow, as I said. About the size of his passport, which he always has with him. Some Chinese-type characters were written on them in black ink. They seemed very old. Some of them were falling to pieces. I suppose that's why he was trying to preserve them. They seemed to have some sort of power over him. He walks around with them in his dressing-gown pocket all the time. And he wears that same old-dressing gown all the time, too. Never changes, you know. It makes me ill just to look at him. I think he relishes this kind of semi-invalid condition.

Dr Z: Did he ever say what these papers were?

F: No, never. He doesn't talk much these days. Just makes his tea and disappears. Sometimes I think he is watching me, you know, observing me out of the corner of his eye. It gives me the creeps. What have I done to deserve this silence?

'There is a gully, sparsely timbered with ironbark-trees. All around there are grey and brown canvas tents. The ground is completely dug up, as though giant rodents camped below while an invading army bivouacked above. Mud and clay suck at our feet. Walking a short distance in this terrain is like making a day's journey along hard ground.

'Horse-drawn wagons are filing out of the camp. My eyes pretend to see nothing but the light in the sky and the fly-speckled back of Tzu, marching relentlessly before me. There is a strange peace in my heart. Something has touched me more deeply than I had expected. Shouts erupt from the hillside. They are taunting us, these white men, desperate for entertainment. I wonder why it is that aggression springs to the surface so easily when men are intent on enjoying themselves? Their drunken voices reel into the hazy sky.

'In the clearing we are stopped, ordered to procure licences. We are designated an allotment of ground below a hill. Running water is three miles away. We are not allowed to use the stream that the whites are using, though we may buy their water for one shilling a bucket.

'The day wears thin. We pitch our tents alongside those that are already there. We meet old friends we have not seen for many years. But it is not with happiness that we speak to one another. There are many tales of hardship and tragedy. Already I have noticed, on the hilltop above our camp, the three graves marked with stones. Such a frail thing, human life; such loneliness, the sunken graves of three old men who survived the journey only to die here.

'Next to the graves a party of drunken men is holding a competition. One of them has a watch in his hand. At his command, the men begin to urinate. They are trying to see who can urinate the longest without a break.'

'Daybreak steals upon us. I am looking forward to the digging. Work is such innocence. It purifies me to swing my pick in the eight feet square of ground, working through the sludge of others, seeing in every grain the dull yellow of my own expectations. It does not take long for the blisters to form on my hands, but I delight in their pain, intoxicated by my work, listening to the rhythm of my comrades: Tzu puffing next to me, Ah Pan groaning behind me, Wang spitting on his hands as though he had to prove he enjoyed an honest day's work.

'We worked long and hard; twelve hours a day. We took turns bringing up the water, two trips per man. We worked the tailings through in the tub, pouring the precious buckets of water in, skimming the sludge off with a shovel. We were digging as well, deeper and deeper. When we struck new ground, we fossicked, crouching down on our hands and knees in the hole, picking and blowing and scratching like chickens.

'For seven days we worked without stopping, except for our two meals at midday and at nightfall. On the eighth day I thought Tzu had been bitten by a snake. He was yelling, rolling around the bottom of his hole like a severed centipede. He was holding something in his hand. Maybe he had gone mad. We hauled him out. There were two specks of gold in his palm.'

'Second week at the diggings. We are working vigorously. It rained all last night and all today, and everything is soaked, including our bedding. The ground is a quagmire. Earthworms ooze through the mud. As we dig and wash in the heavy rain, the air becomes heavy and warm. It is impossible to see farther than our holes. Whenever we put down our shovels and remove our hats we find nests of spiders under the rim. A huge tree cracks and tumbles into the gully. Lightning sparks the hills and a smell of gunpowder sits in the heavy air. Leaves spin down from the trees on the opposite slope. We are shoring up the collapsing walls of our graves. Somewhere down near the stream there is a blast from a gun. Ducks beat the air above our heads.

'Later the same day. Lighter rain is falling now. It is getting cold. In the mist a strange figure darts from tent to tent. I see him now, bandy-legged, moving towards us. He slips and falls in the mud. When he reaches our pits he squats on his heels and begins to talk to us, even though we do not stop our digging.

'"My dear brethren," he says, watching each of us in turn with sharp squinted eyes, a cunning smile creased on his face. (If I hadn't looked twice, I wouldn't have made this qualification. I am no expert on faces, but it seemed that his smile wanted to be read as cunning. It was a mark of his trade. We would have wondered about him if his face were honest and open.) I knew I had seen him before.

'"My brothers and fellow countrymen," he went on, "it is such bad weather. Our labours become more and more in vain under such skies. Each day we dream of our homeland, of our loved ones, waiting for the results of our work here. Your work is difficult, your provisions scanty." We were beginning to feel very sorry for ourselves, but we paid him no heed. "How you must yearn for a warm fire and dry clothing. I can see by your tent that you will need some good canvas; to say nothing of watertight boots and perhaps an oilskin and a good bottle of rum ... all at reasonable prices ..."

'We continued digging, nodding out of politeness, appreciating his unending chatter if only because it took our minds away from our discomfort.

'"If you need any of these things do not hesitate to call in at my store at Creswick's Creek. I sell everything there ... tubs, cradles, even saddles. And if luck favours you, as I hear it has, then I will buy your gold from you. I give the best exchange rates in this part of the country. Of course, I only do this for my fellow countrymen, you who have come all this way to make your fortune, so that your families will prosper, so that China will prosper, China, our homeland that sits in the very lap of Buddha, centre of Tao, gateway to heaven. I can also arrange sea passages, overland coach services, Murray river excursions ..."

'He went on unceasingly. After a while he stood up, thanked us for our time and scampered away to the next group, no doubt repeating the speech we had just heard.

'The evening arrives early. We stop work, glad to be stretching out above our holes, looking forward to the tin of rice Ah Pan is boiling over a dismal fire. I sit heavily on a log beside the fire. Ah Pan's face shines like a lantern above the flickering light. His face is losing some of its boyish innocence with the work he is doing.

'"Who is that fellow who came by today?" I ask him, suspecting he would know his name, having done his water trip more slowly today on account of the mud. I knew that he would have stopped to speak with others.

'"I think his name is Ah Fung, and he owns the general store in Creswick's Creek. The men say that he is a gambler and a cheat, that he took all his wife's money and settled here, leaving her behind with his child," Ah Pan said.

'I knew I had seen his face before. In the half light Ah Pan's face reminded me of that abandoned woman's, appearing out of the depths of the dark shop, holding her baby to her breast. There is the same sadness about it, the same loss of innocence brought on by hardship.

'So my uncle is here, a viper in a nest of vipers, where he seems to be flourishing.'

The task of writing, which must have been almost pleasurable for you, Shan, after your day's physical labour, is for me an agonizing ritual. When I translate your words I feel every pain that custom would not have allowed you to voice. Yet it is this task that is the panacea for my illness, it is this recording process that provides me with a meaning.

I can see your father dimly lit in history, sitting by the window in the early evening when the flowers breathe their secret odours, filing his long nails, reciting his poetry out of an impassioned, painted face.

This love of language is in itself a vice; and at the same time it controls my life. It is fostered and nourished in me by memories such as these; memories, too, of a drowning sister. How peaceful the silence in that swift river!

We will celebrate our lives together. I will not let you, Shan, drown in a wild river. I will bring your words, hermetically sealed, to the light. And as for myself, I shall live the way old people live, in the past, the past which is a dream that has not yet come about, and my life will become infinitely richer.

In the month that Shan had been in Ballarat it had turned cold. He had not counted on its being cold in Victoria. He had brought with him only an old quilt he had had since he was a child. It was not enough to keep out the freezing nights. Lying in his tent, he was alarmed that his teeth chattered, that he could not stop his legs from shaking.

The day came when it was his turn to go for supplies. He put on his straw hat and his torn boots. His clothes stank of old sweat and mud. He had never been able to get used to his own smells, rising from his body like the fetid odour of a swamp, besieging him. He once used to like them, the milder smells of the warm place he occupied in bed, familiar, secure smells.

It was one of those fine, cloudless days that followed a freezing night. He walked slowly, enjoying the sunshine, savouring the morning away from the back-breaking work. There was money in his pocket. He hummed a tune loudly, one of the sons Ah Pan sang which stuck in his mind. His back was warmed by the sun.

Creswick's Creek was different from what he had imagined it to be. It was a canvas town filled with bustling Chinamen. Here and there wooden shanties had sprung up among the tents, evidence of a less itinerant population of shopkeepers. The town even boasted a rudimentary main street, lined with shops that supplied everything from pickaxes to jars of preserved ginger. He noticed that quite a few Westerners were browsing in the shops or standing outside them, examining a cradle for its durability and capability for sifting the sludge from the gold, or testing the strength of an axe or shovel. From one of the shops a sweet smell subtly invaded his nostrils. He had not smelt that in a long time, the Chinese bean curd that would melt on his tongue, flooding his mind with memories of tranquil afternoons in his village when the wandering vendors would set up their stalls in the street, stoke up the fires under the huge pans and then shout their wares in voices worthy of the best opera singers.

He approached the general store at the end of the town. There was a sign outside. It said:

SMALLGOODS AND HARDWARE
SO AH FUNG, PROPRIETOR

He went in. It was dark inside. There was a mixture of smells— herbs and dried pork sausages. A man was sitting behind the counter. He was struggling with some calculation on his abacus, clicking his tongue in time with the clacking of the counters and sighing every now and then at the realization of a mistake. He paused, looked up at Shan and then continued his calculations.

Shan rested his elbow on the counter, glanced around the shop and then said, 'Greetings, uncle. You may not recognize me, but I am Shan, your nephew.'

Ah Fung looked up slowly, confused, the numbers still jangling in his mind. He blinked several times, squinted his eyes, and then continued flicking at the counters.

'So you are my nephew,' he said at last with slow, measured words. He nodded several times. Suddenly he flung the abacus away with a violence that startled Shan, who stood to attention, watching his uncle intently. Ah Fung's face softened, smiled in the same cunning fashion.

'I'll whip that boy,' he said. 'He never brings me the right supplies.'

He motioned Shan to come forward.

'Come, come, nephew. Welcome to Ballarat. As you can see, business is not so good. Too much competition, too much credit and no payments.'

He paused, took a long look at Shan and then continued, 'So you are Shan, my sister's boy. You have grown. How old are you now?'

He pointed at a chair, indicating that Shan should sit in it.

'Twenty-two,' Shan replied.

'Twenty-two,' Ah Fung repeated. 'That is young. All these young men seeking their fortune'.

Ah Fung seemed to withdraw into his thoughts for a few moments. He looked at Shan out of the corner of his eye.

'And how is your mother?' he asked suddenly.

'She passed away about a year ago.'

'Oh. I didn't know.' Ah Fung frowned.

'She was sick for a long time.'

'Yes, I knew that. That makes me very sad. Even though she was my sister I had not seen her for some time—not since the funeral of your little sister.'

Ah Fung sighed. He seemed genuinely grieved. He went behind the counter again, to an iron stove in a corner, and poured some boiling water from a kettle into a delicate porcelain teapot. He brought out two cups from under the counter.

'You know, the gold here has dried up.' He handed Shan a steaming cup of tea.

'I'm telling you this because you are family. I know this for a fact. There's no point looking here. The rush was on a few years ago. Now they're only bringing in a few grains at a time. As shopkeepers, we have to convince them that there's still plenty about. Otherwise we'd have to pack up and move on with them to Bendigo or some other place.'

He settled himself into a chair he had placed opposite Shan. He sighed again.

'Look, I suppose you know about my reputation around here?' he asked, looking carefully at Shan.

'I've heard it said that you're a gambler and a cheat,' Shan said.

'Yes.' Ah Fung seemed relieved. 'Yes, they call me that because I am smart. I keep my wits about me. There are a lot of bullies and thieves around these parts, but I don't let them put it over me. I treat everyone with the same mistrust. Perhaps with the whites I smile a bit more, nod a bit more; but secretly I'm getting the best of the deal. I have to live, too, among cheats and thieves. Do you see what I mean?'

'Yes,' Shan replied.

'But I'm no cheat,' Ah Fung went on. 'I don't rob others. I have a nose for a good bargain. They don't like me because I don't give credit. I don't take risks. These men are gambling without their brains; relying on luck. Luck! A most irrational thing. There's no such thing as luck, if you ask me. That's why I'm not out there digging for gold. The fortune is to be found here.' He waved his arm around his shop. There was a long silence.

'I can see you do not agree,' Ah Fung said.

'I don't know,' said Shan. 'There is the element of adventure, of experience ...'

'Ha! You call the back-breaking work, the sickness and the exposure to the elements, adventure? Experience perhaps. But it is an experience that teaches you nothing. It is worthless. You will die before you realize it.'

Shan looked at him. He had not expected such despairing news from one who had deserted his family and callously sought his own fortune in a new land. He was an adventurer if ever there was one.

'*Découragez les autres*,' the Jesuit had said. The phrase crept into his mind. Perhaps Ah Fung thought that Shan was there for a reason, that his nephew was going to prey upon this blood relationship and that he would have to honour familial ties.

'Listen,' his uncle said. 'There is more fortune to be found here. In this business. Every now and again someone will find a sizeable nugget; one find in thirty thousand holes, and everyone will come rushing back from far and wide—literally. I used to see them running: old men, youngsters, racing for a bit of ground. Fights would break out. Someone would get knifed. A couple of heads would be broken. Whites would sign petitions and mobs of them would form. Trouble would continue until somebody else found a grain or two. Then there would be a bit of peace for a while. Now these people all need equipment, provisions, food, clothing. You could do well here.'

Perhaps he had been wrong about his uncle.

'Are you suggesting I work with you?' Shan asked.

'I'm not suggesting anything. I'm offering you a partnership. You have some money I presume?'

'Not much. An old man died on board the ship. I found some money among his things. As soon as I find out where his family is, I will send it back. I have no money of my own.'

Ah Fung considered this for a while.

'How much is it?' he asked.

'About five pounds equivalent in all.'

'That's not bad for a start.' Ah Fung smiled. 'You could make three times that in a year in this business.'

'It wouldn't be right to use a dead man's money in a business partnership,' Shan said.

Ah Fung stopped smiling. His eyes narrowed.

'Look, you've dishonoured him already. If you subscribed to real honesty you wouldn't have taken it in the first place.'

Shan hadn't thought about that. The money was there. He took it. Somebody else would have taken it. Strange, such recognition of principles coming from his uncle. He felt hypocritical and angry at his failure to face such weaknesses in himself.

'Make it work for you,' Ah Fung said. Tn a year you could send back more than double the amount if you wished. The family would be grateful for it. Look, it isn't just the business in this shop that is profitable. You know there is a large Chinese community up the road a bit, in Bendigo?'

'Yes. I heard the gold was plentiful there.'

'Don't be fooled. It may be more plentiful because there are more people digging for it up there. You'd be lucky to break even. Look, there's a ready market for some things up there.'

'What things?'

'You've seen for yourself how they like opium. I can supply this. Fine grade opium, pipes, everything. They'll jump at it.'

'Where do you get it from?'

'Ah!' said Ah Fung. He didn't answer.

They sipped their tea. The sky outside had clouded over, making the interior of the shop darker. Shan watched the silhouette of his uncle raising the cup to his mouth. Suddenly he spoke, the cup still held to his mouth.

'I'm doing this for you because you're family. I wouldn't make the offer to anyone else. Who can you trust if not your own family? Tell me that. It will be good. We will work together. Think about it.'

'I will,' said Shan. Tn the meantime, could you fill this order?' He took out a slip of yellow paper from his pocket.

As Ah Fung began to fill some sacks with flour, tea, rice and dried fish, his nephew's mind was already on the road to Bendigo.

Fatima stands on the chair in the full splendour of her nakedness. There is abundant light from the window. She could be an apparition: Our Lady, Fatima—except for the fact that her overweight body threatens to snap the legs of the chair. Through the half-open door I see her friend Marietta sitting on the floor. As usual, Fatima complains of having to stand for so long on the chair.

'I'm cold,' she says. 'I'm tired,' she says. 'Let's rest for a while,' she says.

Marietta, lean as a whippet, knits her pencil on the sketch pad. It is her fiftieth drawing of Fatima. Marietta sits on her heels, looking up occasionally. She wears black leotards and her black hair is drawn back in a ponytail. Her thirsty blue eyes drink in the image of Fatima. The two have been lovers for quite some time. Often I see them with their arms around each other sitting on the lounge. They do not speak much, but stare at each other for long periods. One day I walked in on their love-making. Marietta has never forgiven me for that. Fatima simply blushed.

I do not derive any pleasure from watching their relationship develop, and suddenly my moral sensibility is disgusted, I do not know why. It is a sensibility, none the less, that cannot take much violation. It increases with self-denial: without abnegation there is no freedom. So this is what I seek: freedom from relationships, even ones that involve me indirectly. In the hallway mirror I see my reflection withdrawing from the scene; a gaunt old man shuffling away.

The other day Marietta burst into my room. Foolishly I had forgotten to lock my door. She had her sketch book in her hand and there was a fire alight in her eyes. She did a quick sketch of me while I stared at her in bewilderment. Then she went out.

Marietta had an exhibition at the Australian Gallery. There was a series composed of Chinese faces. I appeared in one painting. It was a face full of suffering. My cheeks were sunken, my eyes hollow. I was bald. It was the painting of a skull, consumed from within by several generations of worms. Marietta claimed her paintings formed a historical statement.

Dear X,

The patient [Seamus O'Young] seems to be suffering from a form of paranoid-schizophrenia. He thinks himself to be of another race. Haven't come across this particular one before, so am referring him to you. You'll find everything in the file. A brief summary of the symptoms:

1. Tends to speak of himself in the third person a lot, often in Chinese(?).

2. Sometimes does not speak at all, but writes messages on paper.

3. Reclusive; has a horror of being observed.

4. Is disgusted by the sight of food. (Could be anorexia n.)

5. Believes his wife is having an affair with another woman.

See you when next you come down for some fishing. Caught six fair-sized flathead yesterday—4-lb. breaking strain. Does it make you green with envy?

Looking forward to your diagnosis of the Chink.

Best Wishes,

Z.

'I said goodbye to Wang and Ah Pan. They have chosen to stay behind. Tzu and I packed out belongings and set off on the road to Bendigo in the late morning. I gave Ah Pan my old boots. The poor boy looked lost when we said our final farewells. He stood at the entrance to the tent waving to us. Wang had disappeared somewhere. It was a fine warm day. The sun bounced off the eucalypts, creating a blue tint in the air. As we crossed Creswick's Creek I glanced over at Ah Fung's shop. I thought I saw Wang sitting outside, drinking a cup of tea with my uncle. A stream of people jostled up and down the track. I could not be sure of what I had seen.'

Bendigo: the name of a prize-fighter; the name of a town. Seven Chinese camps nestle in gullies and perch on hillsides. The whites feel threatened by the sheer force of the foreigners' numbers, while the Celestials withdraw more deeply into their centres. The situation is volatile, and two sorts of anxiety can be read on the faces of Westerner and Oriental alike: insecurity and a sense of being outlawed and besieged.

Shan asks to see the head man at White Hills. It is evening, the third since he and Tzu left Ballarat. They are ushered into a large white tent. Large lanterns hang from the centre pole of the tent, emitting a soft, dim light. The old man is sitting on a straw mat. He wears an embroidered silk waistcoat over his long grey gown. His feet are crossed in front of him, wearing black felt slippers. He motions them to sit. He does not smile and there are no words of greeting.

'You have come at a bad time,' he says immediately. 'You are late-comers. Things have soured here. The white man is resentful of us. He is out for blood. Things have gone beyond control.'

The old man sucks at his teeth. He doesn't say any more for a while. It is his prepared speech for those who seek him out and still pay him their respects. He expects them to leave now, but Shan and Tzu look at each other and remain seated. The old man beckons to his son who is standing at the opening of the tent and asks him for tea.

'Things will start to erupt. I can feel it in my bones. You know,' he says, squinting his eyes, 'the young have brought along their old ways ... isn't that strange?' He chuckles to himself. It is a joke he shares only with himself. His face hardens all of a sudden. He looks as though he is grieving. 'They have imposed a

residence tax on us in addition to the digging licences. Do you
know that?'

The two young men shake their heads.

'Oh, yes. And do you want to know something else? We have
to pay for our own protection. Each man will have to pay £4
per year. Special white constables belonging to Her Majesty's
England will protect us. She is a good woman, Her Majesty's
England. I shall send her a letter to thank her, but in it I will say
that £4 is too much for us. Yes, I will do that.'

A teapot and some cups are set before them. The old man
pours and offers his guests a cup. He sighs, and sips his tea with
a loud slurping noise.

'Yes. Things have come to this,' he says. 'Everywhere there
is bullying, bribery, corruption, gambling. If you are good men
you will stay away from certain places. Think of your families
at home ...'

The old man lapses into a dream. He is walking through
corridors of heavy curtains. He parts them, discovers new passages. He walks deeper and deeper into the labyrinth of colour
and sensation. Old memories besiege him. He is tired.

Shan and Tzu bow to the old man. He does not see them
with his glazed eyes as they leave the tent. It is dark now. They
do not know where to go. It is reasonable to assume that they
will make their way to the best-lit, most lively part of the en-
campment, a quarter filled with wooden shacks and food-stalls;
it would not be unlikely that there would be a few women there
too, moving about behind frosted windows, in low-cut dresses,
whirling through the smoke.

Steam and smoke. The night is cold and laughter cracks the
air like hammers on icicles. The mist crowds in over White
Hills. A young man sits in the doorway of a tin shanty. His
eyes are glazed, reflecting the busy firelight. He spits period-

ically, from the side of his mouth. He seems to be very sleepy. In his left hand he holds a bamboo pipe. The night is glazing his eyes with ice; cold, the blood in his veins, the shallow tide of strength ebbing and flowing up to his beleaguered brain; some constituents of character washed out with each wave, and in the sand, the water upturns and draws with it the grains that run back with the wash, and the young man thinks he sees golden specks of sunlight, snowballing into nuggets the size of his fist, heavy as lead to lift, the strength disappearing from his arm with that last wave. Then the nugget was gone for ever, lost in that great ocean of experience until the next time ... the next time ... and now the wave darts back and washes scallops of sand around his feet which are turning blue with cold; and then the wave recedes and in the sand worms a yard long emerge with fantastic rapidity and coil themselves around his feet, and he feels thousands of tiny claws biting into his calf ...

'Fook!' Shan shouts, running up to his former pupil, the one with the mind that harboured once the germ of perhaps a great poet. 'Fook, what are you doing here?'

It is a useless question, Shan. His eyes show no recognition of you, his forehead is cold and yet it sweats. It is best to leave him alone to release himself if he can from the icy clutches of the worms in his mind, hatched from that germ of poetry that once promised so much.

Shan shakes him by the shoulders and, perceiving what seems to be insolence in his expression, lets him flop back against the doorjamb, making the hut boom like a drum.

'If only you could see the misery that surrounds us. Men go to ruin, some because they have found gold, others because they have found none. Beneath the fabric of outward serenity, all social order has disappeared. No, there is no fighting in the streets yet, nor is there blatant drug-taking and whoring. But if you look beyond the smoke, if you cast your eyes about, if you lift up tent flaps, you will see the untrusting and untrustworthy faces of men around gaming tables, you will hear the steady rattle of dice, you will see the listlessness of the drugged, hear their rattling breath as they sniff and cough, their noses like dripping taps; you will see the painted faces of the whores that have just arrived from Melbourne, hear their giggling as men's hands travel up their thighs; while all around you the faces seem impassive, sweating at the gaming table, dreaming of a sleep that will never come, faces which change at night from anxious ones to lustful ones. Asian and Caucasian, men lusting after women, men lusting after men.

'But there is this warmth of human beings, this throbbing life that attracts me, I know not why. Tzu and I are drawn like moths towards a lamp as we smell the food cooking in the pots over the fires, as we see the anticipation of the gamblers, the peace of the drugged, the passion of the debauched. Are we all victims? Is this the dance of death, the revelry amidst the holocaust? Is this the behaviour of ruined men, men who are under threat from within and without?

'What is the aim of all the training of my youth, what is the aim of a life of denial, of a character whose ideal is strength? Is it not for the experience of the world? Is it not through experience that one becomes a Great Man? Is not the bland Confucian man lacking in flesh and bone; a sheltered, privileged, faceless nonentity?'

Location is so important for me. Where I sit. Which window I am looking out. Which room I walk into. Where the sun or the shadows play. It is connected to the process of time, in the same way as memories are connected to moods. I wish time could be a release instead of an imprisonment. Towards the end of the day, in the late afternoon, the anxieties that have been building up in me become too much.

In the library I consult Chinese dictionaries. How does one give meaning to feelings in another language, especially one that is built on images? Are the feelings exact? Are the words exact? I want to feel exactly.

A woman with a pram pushes past the window. A kaleidoscope of colours and shapes filters through the bamboo blinds. It is a movement of unsynchronized frames from an old film across a bamboo screen. Do feelings occur in series, can they form part of the same set of moods brought on by certain images and circumstances? Are feelings the same even if these things occurred more than a hundred years ago? I struggle to the library wash-room like a semi-invalid, my movements unsynchronized.

There I meet an old school friend. I have not seen him since our school days, since those years in the boys' home, decades ago. I recognize him immediately though, as we stand side by side at the urinal. He still has the same close-cropped hair, the same long sideburns. He has not changed since the day I asked him to describe me in the playground. Of course he doesn't recognize me now. He balances on the step at the urinal, as though he was drunk.

'Terry,' I say, 'don't you remember me?'

He looks at me. It suddenly dawns on him.

'Seamus!' he exclaims. 'Seamus O'Young ... well well, well. Fancy meeting you here. Heavens, you've aged!'

We finish urinating. As we wash our hands he says, 'What have you been doing with yourself, then?'

I give him the usual story. This and that. I was a school teacher, I'm married, I write stories, tell tales.

'What about yourself?'

He wipes his hands carefully with his handkerchief and then uses it to turn off the tap. He goes over to the automatic hand-dryer. The noise it makes is terrible, like a jet engine, but it provides a background noise for his muffled answer. After all, someone could have been in the cubicle, listening.

'I'm in the priesthood,' he says softly.

He moved close to me when he said it, as though he was afraid I might have disapproved; or maybe it was a well-kept secret. Perhaps he was thinking of leaving, or was an undercover priest, one of those secular agents from the Vatican, sent out to test the rigidity of the Catholic hierarchy. Even though he wore a checked flannel shirt, I noticed immediately the black trousers and old-fashioned, round-toed black shoes.

We walk out into the foyer. He holds my arm as we walk, steering me over to the circulation desk, grabbing an armful of books. I do not know what to say to him.

As he fills out his cards he asks me suddenly, 'Do you still go to mass?'

'No, I've lapsed,' I confess.

'You once told me you wanted to become a Jesuit.'

'Did I? Hell!'

'Ha, it's not as drastic as that, we hope.' 'You still believe, do you?'

He smiled, as though he didn't really expect an answer. I ventured to supply one.

'I don't know. I've changed. The crisis is there ... when I think about it. I don't know whether it is possible to believe vicariously: that is, one side of me says that I do, the other, I don't. I end up believing through others, you know, a kind of imaginary congregation of worshippers through which I worship. But I'm not making any sense.'

'No, no. I mean, yes.'

'I still feel that the world has spiritual significance, which constantly changes ... you know ... that it's not all historical materialism. I suppose I can't accept dogma. That's why Buddhism interests me, though I'm not a Buddhist. I like the space between thoughts in the Buddhist mind.'

'That's good,' he said. 'That's good.'

I waited at the desk while he picked up his books.

'Yes,' he went on, 'it's language that destroys significance, in the same way that experience destroys love.'

'What do you mean by that?' I asked. It was ludicrous, the two of us standing there discussing such things.

In the spiritual sense, once you say something, it is no longer significant. It's the same with love, only it's experience that most often stands in its way. It denies love its true expression. When you can't express love ideally, it languishes and wilts. When next you confront it, on the other side of experience, you find it alien; and yet it came from you, from your own soul. You wander around with it there, tagging along beside you. Then you'll try to reconcile it to you: and that's when it becomes difficult, impossible.'

Suddenly I knew I was feeling exactly as Shan had felt a hundred and twenty years ago. He was struggling with language and experience. His soul, imprisoned, had sought escape through language. Now raw and potent experience began to destroy the meaning which he had found in pity and humanism and which he had sought to express in his writing. Had he been turning away from real life? Had his reflections, which hinted at his spirituality, been preventing him from acting, from taking the plunge into the secular experience which in this land was a prerequisite for survival? The imagination alone had not enhanced his capacity to 'see'.

I had noticed that his writing no longer sheltered beneath a comfortable lyricism. There seemed to be a tinge of fear in the prosaic, documentary style.

Terry checked out his books and moved through the glass doors. Outside the library we shook hands and wished each other well.

'You know,' he said as he was about to walk off, 'when we were at school together I found out that I loved you. That was when I learnt this thing about experience. I had a hard time of it. Love was abundant. It overflowed from me. And then I realized God was beckoning to me, and I understood that this was a special gift I had which was wasting away. That was what made me join the priesthood.'

He walked off then, disappearing round the corner. It began to rain.

The days grew shorter as they worked and reworked the tailings. They had found a few more specks of gold. A little of the money they got for it began to find its way on to the gaming table. Some of their savings were paid into the Triad Society, which, they were told, would provide them with protection.

They worked the tailings in the new cradle they had bought, the rusting grate swallowing mountains of earth as they rocked it to and fro. A man watched them. He stood up on the hill a little distance away, under a tree. He appeared there every day and watched them for about two hours. They knew he was a white man.

They worked hard; they were unique in the way that they had cut themselves off from the rest of the Chinese diggers, keeping apart, making the nightly pilgrimage into the quarter when they had money. They worked through the heat of the day, pausing only for a brief meal, while white men rested and slept in the shade of trees. They became a curiosity for the whites, who would come over to see whether they had found something, since they were digging so vigorously. The onlookers would stand there, not speaking, getting in the way. Shan and Tzu worked around them, while they drank, spat, cursed and watched until the sun became too hot. The two of them grew faint in the sun and longed for rest; but the days were growing short, and daylight became as precious as gold.

One day during this hot period between noon and three in the afternoon, a small, balding European wearing a pince-nez arrived at their pit. He had with him two companions of large stature with full beards and flushed faces. The small, balding man kicked over their cradle and began to threaten them with a shovel.

'Dis here ist mein verking,' he growled. The men with beards began pushing the Chinamen away. 'You people come here vith no regart for ozers, for to take avay mein gold. Ja, you go if you know vat's gut for you. If you shtay you de heads vill lose, ja?'

He menaced them with the shovel. There was laughter, and other white men began to gather. Shan bent down to pick up the cradle. He was kicked from behind and he sprawled in the mud. Tears of frustration formed in his eyes. A bottle was thrown. It hit him on the side of his face. The two Chinamen ran for their lives.

In the evening they met the leader of the Triad Society. Yes, he had heard about him, this man who wore glasses. He had been robbing, bullying and harassing Chinamen for over two years. A known claim-jumper, his trademark was a banner adorned with Chinese pigtails which he erected over the pits. No one doubted that he was a dangerous madman.

Several weeks later the short, balding man with the pince-nez disappeared from the goldfields. The police rode round asking questions. Mr Mollisson, the resident warden, consulted with the elders. No, nothing was heard about him. Perhaps he had been warned off. The elders shook their heads. Things like this could only lead to trouble.

'We are now bearing the full brunt of their hatred.

Several Chinamen were beaten up in a dispute over water. Everywhere we are accused of wasting water, of dirtying it, of ruining good ground.

'Dear reader, how difficult it is for me to stand in the middle, how difficult it is to remain impartial, to be apart from the fray! It is not a badge that I wear out of choice. My people are not

idealistic men. We do not hoist pennants of defiance. Yet sometimes I feel that this is the only way.

'I cannot help feeling a sense of betrayal, because I know that
it will not be physical hardship on the one hand, or greed and
desire for luxury on the other, that will throw me into the pit of
baser feelings. It will be conscious decisions, rational battles in
my mind. As my teacher once said to me: "If you swerve from
your path, it will be because you have applied thought to the
world, making excuses for it and for men's actions, excuses for
what is happening in the world."

'But I have visions that one day even monks will immolate
themselves in protest against men's actions, and a reason will
be supplied.'

'Water. It is the cleansing substance. They say that we dirty the
water. Thus we are dirty. Yesterday, two Chinamen were horse-
whipped for rolling up their trousers and wading in the stream.
We are accused of spreading diseases. The term most common-
ly used is "leprous". Diseases are seen as evil; thus we are evil.
Yet we suffer from the same illnesses as our accusers.

'Last night there was a raid on one of our camps in the gully.
Twenty tents were burnt. Some men lost everything except the
clothes they wore. The raiders came stealthily, leading their
horses. They threw torches under the tents. Men who were
asleep raced out from the inferno. Some tried in vain to save
their belongings. There was confusion. There were shouts,
galloping hooves, pitchforks ripping through canvas. The fires
lit up the gully, flickering over the trees. They love fire, these
marauding tribes. Fire cleanses, too, rids them of their guilt,
destroys diseases, the vermin of little yellow men.'

In my solitude nights and days drift over me. Time exists only when it is accelerated or compressed; it becomes noticeable then. The small aspects of my days flow into a backwater and then are released, cascading into pools of memories.

I am closer today to suicide than I have ever been.

Fatima has not been home for weeks. I prowl about the house, peering through the curtains at the suburban street, listening for sounds that are unfamiliar. Sometimes I turn on the television. In an advertisement a woman drops a tray of food. I switch off the television. For the rest of the day I wander about the house with a lingering feeling of wanting to clean up a mess on the floor.

It was an unusually hot day for that time of the year. A bee floated lazily among the bottlebrushes. There was a smell of wild honey in the heavy air. Tzu stood mid-stream, the cool water coursing around his shins. He had two buckets on each end of the bamboo pole. With the pole balanced on his right shoulder, he bent his tall frame and let one bucket fill swiftly, until the weight and the current began to spin the pole around. Then he straightened, and then stooped again, this time letting the left bucket fill. He grunted as he made his way back to the bank, the heavy buckets bending the ends of the pole as he stumbled and slipped over the submerged smooth rocks.

He looked up from under his wide-brimmed hat. The wide, flared nostrils of a horse breathed into his face. A bearded man sat astride the horse staring at him. There was anger in his face. He was not a policeman, Tzu knew, because one had come by several minutes before and had demanded his licence. As he stood there with the water dripping from his buckets another horse and rider approached, and then another. He heard garbled voices.

'That's him. The big bastard,' they said. He could not

understand them, or their anger. He tried to walk between the horses. They jostled him. The buckets were only half full now. He made off in another direction. A horse blocked his path. He was struck across the back. He dropped the buckets. Desperation rose like an icy current from the pit of his stomach. He gripped the bamboo pole, shaking loose the buckets. A club thumped between his shoulder-blades. At that moment, staggering from the blow, he saw a gap between the horses. Dropping the pole he began to run. He found the gap. He ran, pumping his long legs, dodging around trees and low bushes. A horse loomed up beside him. He changed direction. Another horse drew up on the other side, then he felt the breath of another at the back of his neck. A rope flew down over his head, tightened around his neck. He reached up to stop it from choking him. The rope dragged him off along a path. Stumbling, running as fast as he could to ease the tension from around his throat, he began to shout. He tried hauling in the rope. The speed of the horse increased. Suddenly he was on the ground. He was dragged over some bushes. A rock split his mouth. They stopped. He lay panting on the ground. The blood tasted like water from the inside of a fish. He was hauled to his feet. Blood dripped into his eyes.

They were off again, pulling him along. His strength left him. Mechanically he ran along after the horses. Anything to ease the constriction of the rope. He was gasping. An animal sound came from his chest. After five miles they cut him loose.

As he lay under a large tree-fern in a dank rain forest, he choked back on some blood and felt a joy pass over him. His pains disappeared. It was as though a door had opened, and he was able to pass safely into a dream. He had never seen such a forest. Trees spread thick branches over his head. His bed of leaves was soft like down. He was warm, asleep. Then a boulder the size of a bucket extinguished the last glimmer of consciousness left in him.

Since moving to Bendigo, Clancy had been watching Shan and Tzu work the pile of tailings for several days. He had seen the claim-jumper take over their pit when it looked as though they were getting some gold out of it. He watched them start work at another site on the other side of his vantage point. He was interested in these two Celestials. They fascinated him because they worked apart from the others. He wondered if they were outcasts. Two Chinamen working alone like that invited attack.

He had not thought about Chinamen before; not seriously anyway. His mind reverberated with the catchcries of the mob. Of course he resented them. They were taking gold out of the country; they were ruining the land, dirtying the water, spreading diseases. They didn't drink, but they had secret vices. They had some kind of power over white women; they were pederasts ... buying boys to suck them off, the bastids.

Apart from these opinions, Clancy thought no more of them. They were a blot on the landscape, but he could ignore them quite easily. They never made much noise; they worked most of the time; gambled, never lazed around much. They abided by the law, had some sort of reverence for old age, kept to themselves. He wondered why they were hated to the point of violence. Something in his intelligence and something in his conscience told him it was wrong. They shaped up for a battle between his feelings and his overwhelming need for acceptance.

He watched the big Chinaman shoulder the pole and buckets. He watched him walk awkwardly towards the stream a mile away.

'Significance in numbers and generality,' he said to himself. 'The brotherhood of all men. But they're not like us. They have lower standards. Standards! Is that arrogance? They only care about survival. Yes, but they're poor men. Better them than mandarins!'

The battle raged. He chewed on a stalk of grass. He resisted the impulse to confront the lone Chinaman burrowing away at the hole. He fell asleep with his hat over his eyes in the hot sun. A bee droned past his ear. He dreamt of Paradise. Gold and honey. He was floating on a river. A blond-haired girl fed him slowly from the bank with a long spoon.

'I have been waiting for almost two hours for the water. Where can Tzu have got to? Normally he is very reliable. Perhaps it's the heat: he's probably dabbling in the stream. But he knows I will be waiting for the water.

'I had an idea yesterday. I thought how good it would be to get enough gold to buy some land, somewhere far away from here—just as Wah did. I could farm it, raise sheep. I don't wish to return to China. There is nothing for me there. If I had gold I could live with resentment. Even though they will resent and hate me, they will respect wealth and ownership. This is the principle I have been working on.

'Today it seems like a fanciful dream. I would have to move mountains to find gold. I'm beginning to regret my rejection of Ah Fung's offer. My way is not so clear now. As my body wears down, the mistakes I have made torment me, they are so magnified.

'Yesterday I thought of gold. Today I am thinking of a woman. The woman I construct in my mind never appears totally. It is as if I tried to create her image in this mud with my blunt shovel.

'I wonder where Tzu has got to. If I leave everything to go and look for him I will more than likely come back and find everything stolen. Especially since that fellow up there is watching every move I make.'

Clancy woke with a start. The bee had nestled in his ear-lobe. He brushed it away quickly. Below the hill the lone Chinaman was sitting on an upturned tub. He was not working. He had his hands on his knees and was staring at the pit. Clancy rose and walked down the hill.

Some Chinamen were working on the next rise, jabbering away in sing-song voices. There was no movement from the white men's side. They were probably snoring under their tents or drinking grog in the large marquee with the word 'coffee' scrawled on the side.

He approached Shan and then stopped. What would he say to a Chinaman? He couldn't just go up to him and ask him how he was. He put his hands in his pockets and kicked over a few stones. He wished he could speak Chinese. Yes that would be a real advantage in this place. He looked around. He felt embarrassed standing there; but nobody noticed him.

He walked towards Shan, pointed at the pile of earth beside him and smiled.

'Have you found any gold?' he asked as a form of introduction which he thought appropriate.

Shan looked up at him. The white man looked like another claim-jumper, smiling his gap-toothed smile. Shan seized the shovel. He was going to be ready this time.

Clancy did not stop smiling. There was a long silence. He sat down on a rock.

A conversation took place between the Chinaman and the Irishman. It was not unusual in those frontier settlements, where men had time to talk, where loneliness sometimes forced men of different races and beliefs together. That one could speak no Chinese and the other little English, did not matter. There was common ground between the two of them. They had met before, when Clancy had yelled at the Chinamen from the top of the rise. He needed to bare himself, to peel back the mask and alleviate his guilt. It was something he could not talk to another white man about. For Shan, there was an advantage in listening, even though he could not understand everything. He contributed nods and noises of assent.

Clancy wouldn't have made much sense even if the Chinaman had understood everything. He wanted to express the ideas of a brotherhood he had crudely formed in his mind; a brotherhood that made no distinctions between race or religion.

'You're no different from the next man,' he was saying to the Chinaman. 'We're all concerned with our own wellbeing.'

He made a speech about the hardships that were confronting them all, how this shared experience should unite them, give all men, white, yellow and black a common cause in forming a new society.

The Chinaman nodded, agreed. 'Velly bad. No gold,' he said. (Shan withdrew into pidgin English. For once language intervened in his emotions. He was not going to compromise himself with grammatical English. Besides, this appearance of ignorance protected him, provided him with a mask.)

'Gold!' Jesus, is that all you fellows think about?' Clancy shouted fiercely. The Chinaman gripped his shovel.

'Look,' Clancy continued. 'Everything is for the taking here.' He pointed to the pile of dirt next to him. 'Every man wants as much as he can take out, and more.' He struggled with his thoughts. 'But I'm not saying it's just you blokes,' he went on. 'With the white man it's the same thing—only he wants more without the same amount of work. Bloody hell, I've known some idlers.'

He paused, produced a pipe and began to fit small rinds of tobacco into the bowl.

'You know,' he said. 'I've been studying you fellows. I've seen the way you work the ground, methodically, in organized groups. Now that's something we can learn from you. You share out what you get among your relatives. It's a brotherhood, you understand. But you're here, not in your own country. You're sucking everything out and putting nothing back in. Now don't get me wrong. A lot of white men are the same. They'll get their gold and go home to England or Europe.' He lit the pipe, sucking in and blowing out for several moments. 'You see, the problem with you is that you look different and your numbers are so great. You can't spread out and merge in. Yes, that's the basic difference.' Clancy inhaled the smoke, staring into space.

'We feeling velly bad,' the Chinaman said. 'Evellywhere white man hate.'

Clancy looked confused, his train of thought interrupted.

'Look,' he said, regaining his composure, 'if only this idea of brotherhood could be enlarged; if only the white man could learn from your methods without feeling besieged, threatened by a close-knit group of competitors, by the authorities, then something good could come out of this society. There's a war here between greed and ideals. That's basically what it is. There's enough idealism to be harnessed, enough of a sense of brotherhood to make it work. But we've got to break down the distrust. Everyone must accept each other and care. We've got to communicate, organize.'

Clancy's eyes were lit with a zeal. He felt messianic. Before his eyes he saw a park filled with men nodding assent at his words. He tottered on his soap-box with emotion.

'We velly hungly, too,' the Chinaman said.

'There's been a lot of talk about an Australia, a country, a united Australia Felix,' Clancy went on, his voice rapturous, trembling. 'Yes, that's my ideal. It's waiting to be created. A pastoral paradise without greed or fear.'

'We velly cold, velly far flom home.' The Chinaman's voice rang out like a wolf's lament.

Thoughts flew in and out of Clancy's head. The mob in the park filtered away. His soap-box became a mound of slippery mud. What did these words matter to a stony-faced Chinaman? Yet in some strange way he felt he was understood. The Chinaman looked lonely and isolated, a human being like himself, lost in the current of ignorance that was sweeping the goldfields. Good, thinking men were dead, massacred at Eureka, stamped into the ground by the forces of stupidity and self-interest.

'A few years ago we were on the brink of a great possibility. Now that is gone for ever,' he said. 'Now I am a hunted man, John Chinaman, as lonely and as desperate as you are.'

He stood up, knocked his pipe on a rock and walked away, hunched into his thoughts. Shan stared at his back. The wind was coming up now, filling the silence. Centuries of human history had sparked one small covenant in the souls of two men for a brief moment. The wind prevented the spark from catching.

NOTICE

There are several ways of deterring the voluptuous, sensual, immoral CELESTIAL and getting rid of him: that is, if you are CHRISTIAN and you care about your woman and children. You are MORALLY JUSTIFIED in driving out the hated HEATHEN. You can:

1. Pull off his pigtail if on horseback.
2. Hang him head down over a mine shaft.
3. Run him behind your horse with a rope around his neck.
4. Burn his tents.
5. Stand him on a bucket and nail his ears to a tree.

If the Chinese could have read the notice they would have been terrified. It hung from the wooden wall of the house of debauchery. Standing outside, they would have been fascinated by the warm yellow light that came from the windows. Women moved across them, followed by peals of laughter, tiny bursts of giggling rolling like marbles over the wooden floor. Bearded Irishmen guffawed their way to bed. Silken flurries ... perfume. Practised soprano shrieks. In elegant high-pitched moans from great bear-like men in climatic walks over high-tensioned wires, harbingers of the fall, deep, deep, into black nothingness.

There were girls here who would hire themselves out to men for one shilling and sixpence a day; clothing and food supplied. They had been following the men from goldfield to goldfield. They knew all the things there were to know about making men happy. They accompanied eccentric, lonely men who kept finding gold.

Mary Young strode across the room in her long-legged fashion. She poured some water from a pitcher into a basin. She took a bottle from a shelf, mixed some of the coloured fluid with the water and pushed her long red gown apart. She straddled the basin, holding her gown around her thin waist with one hand, and proceeded to wash herself, dabbing at the blond pelt with a sponge. While she washed she bowed her head over the table, letting her long hair fall over it. There were still grains of gold dust she could collect, tiny grains falling from her hair. Her previous client had been a generous man.

There was a knock at the door. She finished off her washing.

'Hang on,' she called. Her voice was tuneful. She wrung out the sponge, drew her gown around her, went to open the door. A Chinaman stood there, his pigtail over his shoulder.

'No Chinese allowed here,' she said, shaking her head, attempting to close the door. 'Go away from here. They will catch you.'

She waved her hand at him. His face looked sad. It was a sensitive face. She had seen it before. Was it at Ballarat? She began to smile at him. She opened the door for him.

'Hello. My name is Shan,' the Chinaman said in perfect English.

4 SANCTUARY

Are my eyes failing me? Has Shan begun to descend the other side of the mountain, the Big Mist Mountain, the Tai Mo Shan of his mind and his will? Can the real reason for this obscurity be his abandonment of the monastic life? Except for the glimmer of images, what else is left now? In my premature old age I am done with clarity. I think only of ironies.

I have taken such care with the reconstruction of Shan's existence. I have had such faith in his moral uprightness. Now his actions betray me; actions over which I have no control.

I am sunk in a kind of paralysis. I wander through the dark house in search of a sanctuary from myself. How futile it is to seek salvation through writing!

The only brightness in my life comes when Mrs Bernhard, my neighbour, pounds on the door to bring me a batch of scones she had just made, or a basket of fruit she had picked from her own trees that surround her house and form a natural boundary between our properties.

Mrs Bernhard is a widow of about forty. She used to live on a property near the old goldmines at Hill End. One day three years ago her husband went out in the truck to fight a fire that had sprung up in an adjoining property. The truck carried a huge galvanized-iron water-tank. When Mrs Bernhard and several others looked for him later in the day they found a charred black shape under the overturned truck. Mrs Bernhard could not scream or make sounds of grief. There was a deep gurgling in her throat, a kind of croaking. She became mute.

When she comes to sit with me I do not talk much to her,

and she is incapable of producing one single word. But I am tired of hearing my own voice scrape the inside of my skull like a dried leaf against the windowpane on a windy autumn day. Mrs Bernhard butters my scones, pours my tea. She makes little sounds, urging me to eat and drink, pushes my elbow gently. But I have neither the heart nor the stomach for it. I sit and listen to the kitchen clock working out its own madness.

At precisely four o'clock in the afternoon Mrs Bernhard leaves. She has a sense of timing that is in-built and intertwined with her sense of propriety. The moment is always carefully prepared for and chosen with an elegant movement of her head, as though she were listening to the distant chime of bells from an old clock tower. Sometimes, upon leaving, she touches me lightly on the head. It is her parting gift.

For just a brief moment her lingering fingers fill me with a warmth; then I feel the cool breeze come through the door and darkness seemed to descend again.

Again I begin a headlong descent into the past. This is my vice, something I shall soon eliminate: these long glissandoes of prose from another time.

Mrs Bernhard looks at me with her attractive eyes; greyish, greenish, like the sea on dull days; her dark hair drawn across the side of her face. Sometimes when we sit side by side on the sofa she pouts and her red lips try to form words; and I feel how impossible everything is and something in my memory will not make the necessary connections. I sigh. Her long shapely legs are crossed, the expression in her eyes exacting ... or cajoling? There is a faint scent of irony of which I feel we are both aware. I do not dare to act without words. It is a daunting scenario. But an old man of experience would laugh. At precisely four o'clock we wrap up our sentimentalities and the play is over.

He held on to her wrists. In front of his face Mary Young's pear-shaped breasts topped with two dark cherries waggled deliciously. He ran his hands along her sides, cupped them. Above him, her long mane showered him with gifts. His sweating face was sprinkled with gold. After he had fallen into those black depths, while he lay there catching his breath between a sense of loss and the undulating waves of sleep, he felt also the sharp point of his pen inscribing the word 'but' on his heart.

She looked across at his face. It had lost its inscrutability. He looked defenceless, his face like that of a boy caught stealing apples in his neighbour's orchard. His pigtail lay coiled like a snake about his ear, the red string tying its end a forked tongue.

'I saw you when you came into Ballarat,' she said. He did not speak.

'I was with a man I lived with for a year. You might remember him, a bearded fellow. He shouted at you. Sometimes he was like that—an unreasonable man, an animal.'

She spoke softly. He found her voice soothing; it filled the emptiness. He tried, but not with a great effort, to make sense of her words. It was as though she were speaking to him from the rim of a well, and he was at the bottom of it, looking up at her, hearing those strange sounds cascade down to him like droplets of water.

'His name was Clancy. That's not his real name. He had to change it to avoid the joes. They were after him for a long while after Eureka. I suppose you've heard of Eureka.'

The name was familiar. He gave no indication that he had.

'He was accused of being among the ring-leaders,' she continued. 'They said he incited the men to riot. He was with another fellow, an Italian called Carbono or Carboni, I don't know which ... the two of them were inseparable. They were always talking about "great works". Clancy still carries around a book written by this cove. Sort of a revolutionary testament. Of course the Italian got nicked and Clancy made off. He changed his name and grew a beard. You couldn't tell him from the other diggers, they all look so alike, anyway. So Fitz (Fitzpatrick was his real name) was a hunted man and kept out of the way. He called himself Clancy and became a shepherd when things got hot on the fields. I used to think he took up with me to keep the heat off, if you know what I mean. He turned into a harmless, ignorant shepherd living in a bark hut with his wife, Mary Young, the former darling of high society in Melbourne. All set to marry a gentleman farmer, I was.'

She peeked over at Shan again. His eyes told her that he was following what she was saying.

'Well, I couldn't live with him, you know. He was always so full of depression, moping about feeling sorry for himself. He never recovered from Eureka. He used to walk around as though he was dragging a team of horses. I really don't know why I stayed with him so long. One day I just couldn't stand it any more, so I told him he should go off and marry his dago friend, see if I care. He'd be better off talking politics and crying over a mug of rum. I told him it was no man's life, hiding like that, brooding over the past.

'Things got real bad after that. He got savage; took a whip to me one day. I packed my bags and came here. I've got good friends in this business. I have a suspicion he's on my trail this minute, following me around like a dog, begging forgiveness. He couldn't ask too many questions. Someone would stumble to the fact that he was a wanted man. A lot of blokes would turn him in if they knew there was a reward. Trouble is most of them can't read.'

She turned to look at Shan again. He appeared to be fast asleep. Outside the rain was beginning to fall, the wind gusts stabbing at the window with metallic drops.

'Will you come away with me?' he asked suddenly in a tremulous voice. 'I can't be happy, you living like this.'

He didn't know why he was saying it. The words were alien on his tongue. He reached over and touched her hair, twirling lengths of it around his fingers.

She thought for a long while and nodded, though she did not say that it would cost him at least two shillings a day. She did not ask herself why she did not refuse him. He was attractive, determined, caring. Her experience of men had taught her to be wary, but it also assured her that this man was honest. He wouldn't cheat her. It was one hazard of her profession that she could safely remove. Besides, she had to get away from Clancy. She knew what the consequences would be, living with a Chinaman. The thought of Clancy's riding hard after her to deliver her from this mysterious and exotic heathen thrilled her with a sense of romance culled from the cheap novels she had read to fill in those times at the whorehouse when she had her periods.

'You can renounce everything except mortality.' I suspect that thought was in Shan's mind that night as he trudged back to his tent in the rain. He thought of the way he had moaned. He was ashamed of his childish voice. That had also sounded like the groan of a dying man. In the act of life there was also a death.

Dr X: In cases such as this it is imperative that we get a picture of how others see him. I hope it will not be too tiring for you to write some of your opinions down for me.

Mrs. Bernhard: No. I will try to be as candid as possible.

Dr X: Thank you. We are most grateful. Does he seem depressed to you?

Mrs B: No, not at all. He seems cheerful most of the time. There have been times when his mind seemed to be elsewhere, when it would be hard to distract him.

Dr X: Does he ever confide in you? That is, does he ever tell you his feelings?

Mrs B: No, never. He is a very private man in that sense. He has talked about things that mattered, things that seemed important to him at least; but I always got the feeling that they could just as well not have mattered at all.

Dr X: How do you mean? What are some of the things he talked about?

Mrs B: Well, things that pertain to racism and sexism. He once said that the two were inter-related, having to do with attitudes of inferiority and superiority. Not a new idea, mind you. Sometimes he would talk for the two of us, assuming certain opinions to be mine. Needless to say, they did not resemble any of my opinions at all.

Dr X: What were these opinions he attributed to you?

Mrs B: Oh, opinions that attraction between the sexes of different races stem from certain racist and sexist assumptions; that no satisfactory relationship can result unless these assumptions have been overturned.

Dr X: Didn't you agree at all with that?

Mrs B: No, not at all.

Dr X: I see. This leads me to another question that you may find embarrassing. You may decline to answer it if you wish. Has he ever made advances towards you? I mean, of a physical nature?

Mrs B: Of course not.

Dr X: I see that you have underlined this. Are you indignant that I should ask that question?

Mrs B: No. I merely wished to emphasize that nothing of the kind has passed between us. After all, he is a married man, even though his wife left him. I enjoyed his company because he was *sympathique.* Perhaps that isn't the right word. He leads a monastic life. He hardly eats. If I didn't come round with some food he would probably starve.

Dr X: Does he ever talk about death or suicide?

Mrs B: No, except that he mentioned a friend of his called Sham or Shan, whom I suppose he was close to in the past, who had died. He seemed very disturbed by this person's death.

The man and the woman made their way in a north-easterly direction. They had acquired a light cart and a horse. The man walked, leading the horse. He was dressed in trousers tucked into high boots and a coat made from rabbit skins. He had a felt hat on his head. The woman huddled down in the cart wrapped in a blanket. The weather had turned extremely cold. The sky was overcast and it looked as though it might snow. They passed several freshly filled graves.

At night they camped under trees, holding each other under their blankets, their teeth chattering, trying in their half-sleep to spark each other's passion, for warmth, each time falling back exhausted, waiting for dawn and the sun. Under the blanket, the man felt her restless breathing against his chest, tensed himself as she tossed.

Sometimes he would sit up in the night, light the paraffin lamp and try to write, his brush slapping clumsily over the paper. He was unable to form the characters with any degree of skill, his cold hand bunched and misshapen like a leper's stump.

Music. It flows over me, under me, in and out. Mrs Bernhard dances on the edge of my vision, naked. I see shapes that resemble breasts, fleshy arms that hold them bunched like basketful of scones. Music. The black hair flowing over me. Outside the insects are singing. A foot passes before my face. Thighs. An abdomen. I smell her, a faint whiff of Johnson's Baby Powder. She twirls past me. The cleft in her thighs. Shadows are passing over the gully.

They forded the river, made their way through the mountains, through brisk snow showers, blinding hail. They passed groups of silent, exhausted men, ice encrusted around their large straw hats. Then groups of white men appeared and stopped them, circled the cart, spoke to Mary, smiled, spat, eyed Shan suspiciously. They respected the shotgun cradled in his arms. Then it got even colder, and Chinamen and Westerners passed without a glance at them, each man too involved in his own fight against the cold.

It was the prelude to a devastating winter. Already the streams had frozen, sometimes so quickly that waterfalls froze in mid-flight, the ripples of water caught like rows of silver fish, revealing behind the crystal curtain bright green moss or purple flowers seeking refuge in the grotto from the merciless wind. And then the whiteness became a blinding monotony, seeping into their brains, until the broken rhythm of the horse slipping brought them back to concern with direction, or prompted starched and brittle one-word conversations.

'Things move in and out of focus as though I were in a fever, everything blurred like the heat above the fire, though in the centre of the fire things are sharp and painfully clear. And the words I'm trying to translate, crawling like ants across the page, renounce their own responsibility so that I am left to create meaning out of them from my own head.'

Dr X blew his nose into a big white handkerchief and studied the result.

'It's the aging process,' he concluded, pocketing his deposit. 'I'll give you something to make you relax ... and rest your eyes; keep them closed.'

They came down below the snow line, crossed another river and plodded through thick mud towards a range of hills. They had gone for almost two weeks without having seen another human being. Now, gradually, life began to declare itself, blotchy movements of men dark against the hills; miner's tents ballooning in the wind like mushrooms after a brief storm.

In the late afternoon they rounded the last hill and stood looking down at the huddle of wooden huts smoking vigorously in the wind while the sun struggled weakly in the western sky, its warmth only in the imagination. They fought their way down against the wind, leaning on each other, their horse coughing and wheezing with each step, the sound of icicles cracking in its lungs. They found the wooden building at the end of the street.

'Are you sure this is the place?' Shan asked nervously.

'Don't you worry. I worked here once,' Mary replied, pushing back her hair, straightening her long dress. Her face looked ravaged. At times Shan would watch her face, find certain angles and profiles that taught him something about her. He knew none of her experiences, found her spirit daunting. Yet he was not prepared to ask questions, preferring the flow of events to the searching curiosity, the quest for meaning that once was the foundation of his integrity, that poor edifice lying in ruins at the base of his soul.

The door opened. The hubbub of voices exploded from within. Thick smoke smarted their eyes. A large woman appeared in a tight satin dress, her fleshy arms bunching her oversized bosom which, with each breath, rocked a tiny golden locket.

'Fatima!' Mary exclaimed, flinging herself now on the powdered cradle, fleshy arms pushing around her. Shan saw a masklike face come towards him over Mary's shoulder, smiling with ruby lips; eyes which, though wrinkled in glee, were examining him carefully.

'Welcome back, dear,' the face said, making kissing noises. 'Mary Young, for God's sake, I never thought I'd see you again. What bloody misfortune brings you back here?'

Before Mary could reply Fatima grabbed Shan by the arm, breathing hot whisky breath into his face.

'I knew it,' she said. 'You've gone and got yourself a Chinaman.'

Shan was enveloped by a pair of massive arms. He felt rejected and accepted at the same time, like a child being examined by a foster mother the first day in a new home.

Fatima talked incessantly, ushering them along the hallway with elephantine gestures and lumbering effusiveness. In her room she plied them with questions and drinks. Shan was relieved not to have to do much talking. He was very very tired. Mary and Fatima continued their conversation late into the night.

Lulled by the sound of their voices, Shan drifted off into sleep. He did not know whether he was dreaming. He was walking through corridors. Red curtains hung loosely down over the archways, reminding him of a Chinese palace he once visited to the north of his province. Fatima was showing them to a room at the end of the hall. He was unsteady on his feet. Outside the windows he could see the snow falling. It was black against the windowpanes. He passed a sign on the wall. It was carved out of wood in elaborate letters:

BUFFET

As he passed the buffet, Shan saw groups of men and women standing and sitting round card tables. Through the wood and tobacco smoke he saw a young Chinese boy serving drinks. As the boy stopped to collect empty glasses a man seated next to him passed his large hand over the boy's buttocks. The hand was caressing, obscene. Shan felt ashamed. Fatima smiled, and a candle flame seemed to dart from her mouth. As he walked to their room, Shan thought he recognized the boy's face behind the grease-paint and exaggerated eyebrows. Could it have been Ah Pan, the boy who used to sing songs in the pits? But such coincidences were impossible. His mind was exhausted, his imagination stretched by the strange twists and turns of his journey.

Thirty miles back along the trail they had taken, a man was pitching a tent in the darkness, hollowing out the snow with a shovel while his horse pawed the hard crust for meagre slivers of grass. The smoking fire he had built cast enough light over the ground to reveal clues that others had passed this way ... blackened, half chewed bones; human faeces encased in ice.

Lo Yun Shun: Shan's full name. Loosely translated, it means 'old person mountain'. I juggle the words in my mind.

Each day now I am preparing. I am full of energy because I have made a decision. I list what I shall need: a tent, jerrycan, tinned food, shovel, Primus stove, knife, sleeping-bag, air-mattress. Each day I make eliminations. Yesterday I discarded the lantern and torch. Today I have eliminated binoculars and maps from the list.

Shan went out and got his licence the next morning. Mary stayed in bed and Fatima came in to keep her company. As he stood in the queue in front of the commissioner's office, he saw the bedraggled shapes of his countrymen around him, he heard their voices. It was like returning from a foreign country. When he stopped thinking in English it was as though a heavy door had opened, and once again he could see into himself. The introspection was horrendous. Where did his loyalties lie?

He watched their eyes. They shifted like flies from his face when his own fell on them. He saw their rags, their desperation and their hope in the holes of their coats. In the gale that rushed down the main street, wooden signs flapped like vultures above them. Storekeepers unboarded their shops, standing awhile to gape at prospective customers; harnessing poor illiterate men to things they couldn't do without and couldn't afford. He could not stand there, well-dressed, in the company of men who were enslaved.

He left the queue. He wanted solitude. He yearned for the road, the continuing journey: in the process of that journey he could not be touched, could not be reviled by his conscience. Was this because he was too secure, because Mary Young had given him money instead of asking any from him? Or was this because he had a purpose for the journey, knowing that at the end of it there was a vision of the future, a purpose that was far more pressing than any gold mountain? His mind was filled with urgency. His steps became quicker. He saw the large hairy hand moving along Mary's back; he heard her squeals of delight, genuine or feigned; he didn't care. He rushed back to Fatima's.

Mary was having her breakfast. The smell of fried eggs and coffee made his stomach growl. He told her of his plans. She was not happy about travelling again; but he sensed that she would not put up too much of a fight. He said that he was not happy in this place; there would be no gold here. He did not want her to return to her old profession.

'But if I didn't, how would we live?' she asked.

He talked about the Burrangong.

'Where is that?'

He said it was farther north and much warmer. She was not very interested. He talked about leaving on his own. He was in a temper. She knew his determination. She had to think about it, she said. He told her he had heard that Clancy was in town: Clancy, also known as Fitzpatrick, with gaps between his teeth.

Edna arrived in the early evening wearing a bush hat low over her eyes. I had not seen her for a long time. She drove a dirty Volkswagen. I thought she was going to plough straight into the back of my car. I was making my preparations; discarding almost everything now from the boot, leaving only the tent and the sleeping-bag. The VW blurted out a sharp note and came to rest inches from my shins.

She had not aged a day. She shook hands with me formally and then, grasping my hand in both of hers, she pulled me towards her to deliver a waxy kiss on my cheek. She said she was on her way home. She had been overseas. She had picked up the car in Queensland.

'Might as well see Australia, too,' she said.

I led her inside. She was talking all the time. She was sorry she couldn't warn me of her arrival, but had decided only at the last moment to come this way. I assured her that everything was OK. Of course she would have to stay as long as she liked. She would not have known that she had interrupted my plans.

She walked into the dark house, snapping on the lights. One of the bulbs blew. 'Oh, well,' she said, and laughed. She sat opposite me in the sitting-room while we drank several glasses of brandy. She kept her hat on all the time, speaking animatedly with her hands, sitting straight on the sofa, her face twitching with excitement about all she had to tell me. Sometimes she paused, looked around, breathed in deeply in order to find out something about my life. She inhaled the atmosphere, sought out the metaphysical elements of another life, one that had seemed, I suspect, always closed and silent to her.

We had dinner. There wasn't much. She went out to the VW, returned with several bottles of brandy and a basketful of fruit. We dined on that. As I switched off the light she had left on in the garage, I looked across at Mrs Bernhard's place through the apple-trees. I saw her pass across the window; then her light went out.

Edna had the guest-room. She wanted an early night; she was tired from all the travelling. She would tell me more about her trip tomorrow. She installed herself in the room bundled up in blankets reading *Lady Chatterley's Lover*. She had her brandy on the floor beside the bed. Her long, silver-grey hair flowed down on each side of her. I thought of an old folk tale. I saw Edna in a tower, letting down her hair, waiting ... for ever.

Burrangong. June 1861. A place called Lambing Flat. It was a Sunday afternoon. In the light drizzle a mob attacked the Chinese tents.

Before then there had been talk of ejecting the Chinese from the goldfields. Speeches were made outside churches; rallies took place. Notices warning the Chinese were put up; they were written in English.

A brass band led the mob into battle. They spurred their horses into the tents. There were shouts. Confusion. A fire was started. Men were running in all directions. A horseman picked up a Chinaman by the pigtail at full gallop. It was skilfully done, except that the pigtail came off in his hand. A Celestial was bowled head over heels by a blow from a club swung like a polo stick. The rain smelt like blood. Old men and cripples were trampled by horses.

One of the leaders of the mob, a gap-toothed Irishman, kneed his horse into a struggling shape under piles of canvas. He whooped with pleasure. Cruelty, he noted at the back of his mind, was like an itch. The more you scratched, the itchier it became.

The band played on.

My vision has been getting worse. I seem to be looking through a honeycomb, the hexagonal cells imprinted on my retinae. The pages of my passport appear reinforced with chicken-wire, having the effect of making my writing cramped and disordered.

It is an unusually warm morning, and Edna and I are driving to the bush. She is chatting about her trip, driving erratically with a half-eaten apple in one hand and steering with the thumb and forefinger of the other. The VW bumps and slides along the narrow track and there is a smell of smoke in the air. Near the lookout the track ends, so we get out and she leaps over rocks and waves her arms about as we make our way past the small waterfall.

'How superb!' she says when she sees the waterfall. She claps her hands in glee like a child. She tests the pool of clear, cold water with her foot. Then she undresses, though I warn her there may be other people about. She says she will only be a minute. I continue along the track.

'You'd better wait until I'm finished,' she says. 'Or do you know the way?'

It would have taken too long to answer her. It was easy enough to follow the track, and I knew the area well. I could still make out shapes and was not likely to fall off a cliff. From the rise I look back and see her floating in the pool. She does not move. She is a white waterlily. It is strangely silent without her voice. After a while I hear her behind me. She is wet and breathless, and licks at the water falling from her hair.

She was in Hong Kong. There was an incident. She had met a man there, fallen in love, so it seemed. It was a blur in her mind.

'He came up to me in the foyer of my hotel,' she says. 'I think I was having a gin. The air conditioners weren't working. It was terrible, Hong Kong. So humid; such a crush of people. He was neatly dressed, in a white shirt and slacks. He said he knew something about what I was seeking and so of course I was intrigued. He held my hand; said I should have made inquiries from him in the first place. He was extremely good-looking. A tall Asian, well-spoken.'

She thinks awhile, listens. There are only our footsteps. She continues. 'He said he worked at the Central Registry of Births, Deaths and Marriages. He had seen me there; had heard of my inquiries. The next day he took me to lunch in a beautiful restaurant overlooking Repulse Bay. We had lobster. He did not drink. While I was having my dessert he excused himself. I waited for about an hour. He had disappeared. I never saw him again. No one had heard of him at the registry office.'

We arrive at the lookout. 'It's beautiful!' she exclaims. The wind roars against the escarpment. I am caught in that roar; then I distinguish her voice again.

'I did find out something while I was there.'

'What?'

'Your name. I found your real name.'

'My father's?'

'Your paternal ancestor's. The name was Sham ... or something like that. I could only obtain it through word of mouth. There has been nothing written down. Most of the records were destroyed in the war. They were a clan of Tongs, these people, from Kwangtung province. You know about them, I suppose ... a secret society.'

Sham; Shan. I tossed the words to the wind. The resemblance was no coincidence. Sham. I searched my memory. It meant 'clothing'. I heard the sound of the words brought back by the wind. Sham. Sham. Muffled. Clothed. Covering the sea of green trees stirring below. Shadows. Seamus. Seamus.

They arrived in the Burrangong in July. A lot of the Chinese, fearing for their lives, had departed. Everywhere they heard stories of horror. Men were destitute. Their gold was taken. They could not afford the fare back to China. Some were starving, eating only berries and roots they found in the bush. Others were fed by kind farmers who then made them indentured labourers, working for food and shelter. The most unfortunate hired themselves out to sharp-shooting entrepreneurs, and found themselves on the way to the Northern Territory where they lasted a year or two labouring in horrifying conditions, to perish with a dream of returning still pulsing in their minds.

In his tent, late into the night, Shan helped draft a document for his people, petitioning for recompense. Mary Young lay on the camp bed in a deep depression. She watched the falling and rising of her swollen belly. She heard the soft sing-song voices of the Chinamen as they sat by the lamp around the small table. She had not expected this child.

It was so sudden, the morning that she felt ill. She did not know much about pregnancy. In the past she had gone regularly to a doctor who treated her and assured her that she could not fall pregnant. He said she was sterile. She knew that her friends knew ways of getting rid of the unborn. Yet when it came to her she rejoiced. She would struggle through. She was optimistic. It was the sort of optimism that led her to follow Shan; at least she liked to see it as such. She buried her unconscious motives beneath reminders of the way she had been treated by other men.

Yet she did not know anything about Shan's love for her, whether it was 'real' in the Western sense, whether his emotions were whole and not disparate like his words. He had never said he loved her. He told her once that if he said it the emotion

would be gone. But he had shown a real kindness, a real affection that was difficult to disguise, and she took heart from the
struggle she saw on his face; his attempts to mask his sponta-
neity with seeming indifference, till the mask would crack at
the edges and reveal total confusion and embarrassment.

And he was silent. She loved his mystery. She loved searching his thoughts, following their irregularities. She would always discover something she would never have thought of, and
it would have an amazing wisdom and rationality in the long
run. This she liked. It made her secure. For the first time in her
life she did not want anything from a man. Now he had given
her a child. Did he mean to? Did he want to? He expressed no
discernible joy or sorrow upon hearing the news.

But now she was depressed. She did not know why, as she
watched her rising and falling belly, as she glanced over at the
waxen faces lit with a yellowish glow, why she felt his sudden
abandonment of her when his countrymen were around him;
why she suddenly felt such an alien. She had always had good
friends, women she could rely on for anything; she had never really been alone. Women like Fatima mothered and cared
for her. She had never found such affection in men. She had
known big, powerful men; men who instilled in her a sense of
fear, men like Clancy, whose depressions were always beneath
the surface, ready to be blamed on her. She had been hardened
by these experiences.

Shan was different. There was no aggression in him. He accepted whatever happened to him with a kind of fatalism that
withstood anything. She knew he had entrusted this fatalism
to her, almost as if for safe-keeping. She directed his life, she
thought. She felt responsible for his restlessness. This caused
her depression.

She remembered what Clancy had said to her once: 'To be
responsible is to be an alien, to be alone.' She thought of other
things he had said. Clancy had loved her with a jealousy that
thrilled her and stifled her. She felt sick thinking about it.

It was getting cold. The voices had not stopped. She sighed and touched the mound under the blanket.

Desperate armies are making incursions into my solitude. Bulldozers are moving into the area, reclaiming the house. Trees topple down around me. I am besieged; I am a husk, eaten from the inside out. My head aches.

Edna left the next day. She gave me a present, a thing she got from the highlands in New Guinea. It looked like a cow's horn. It was hollow, like something frontiersmen wore around their waists for gunpowder.

'It's a penis gourd,' she said to me through the open window of her VW as she drove off. I waved to her with it in my hand.

I went back to my preparations. I filled the car up with petrol from an eleven-gallon drum. I inflated the tyres: too much better than too little.

He knew he was crazy, dragging her around in her condition. He knew he was crazy, seeing gold lining the road. He knew he was crazy, taking advantage of her because she was tied to him and couldn't do much without him now. He knew he was crazy, loading up the cart and buying a new horse with what was left of their money. He knew he was crazy, dreaming of the pastoral life. He knew he was crazy, making decisions about their future, planning for it, fitting everything in rationally. He knew he was crazy, making life a series of plans. He knew he was crazy when he found out that life wouldn't adjust to his ideas of reality, when he discovered its intransigence, its unwillingness to coincide with his desires. He knew he was crazy when he felt the demands of his body. He knew he was crazy when he heard a voice in him calling for help, when he was blinded by every rock, every stone, every pool of water, blinded by a golden light.

He knew he was crazy when he left her in the tent, this time at
Hill End, went down to the Turon river and saw the gold spar-
kling under the water; when he took his pan, squatting under
the she-oaks hour after hour, and filled a bag with something
heavy, taking it out to stare at it and not believing it was gold,
comparing the nuggets with rocks, and not being convinced.

What was worse, he knew that he was going crazy.

I wake early. It is still dark when I ease the car out of the garage,
release the handbrake, give a push and jump in. The car rolls
to the bottom of the drive. I do not want to wake Mrs Bernhard.
When I try to start the car, it takes three or four turns of the
ignition key. The noise is unbearable. At the fourth turn the car
jumps to life. Mrs Bernhard's light flicks on. I back the car out
of the drive. Through the badly misted rear window I think I
see Mrs Bernhard hurrying out of her house with a basketful
of scones, her dressing gown flapping round her red fluffy slippers. The car accelerates and she disappears. Rubbish-bins line
the street, silent sentinels of civilisation. Arching cats unwind
from the night's work.

I feel an intense joy. The mist is lifting. The road begins to
look sharper, clearer. With the speed of the car, time is compressed. The road winds through the mountains, then dips into
green valleys sprouting large sandstone houses. Behind me the
sun is rising.

Shan walked out into the river, feeling the slippery rocks
with his feet, the cold numbing them; and when he fell the pain
was deep inside of him. Where the water was rushing most in
the narrow neck, he found deep holes and he sank to his waist,
clinging to reeds, and he felt the current drag at him with a
force that lulled him and tempted him not to fight it.

The car rushes on into this hole in my senses. Billboards
beckon me, tempting me to rest in soft beds, in quiet bars of

luxurious isolation. But my mission has begun. The historical moment is near. I am a myth, rushing God-like to the salvation of the man. The plains stretch out before me. The wind rocks the car. Once great forests grew here, holding the sky, creating its form with the shapes of leaves.

He let himself be swept along. In the bend the rushing water rolled him over, and he saw at the bottom of a deep hole, lying on the sand, his sister; and knowing it was a dream he tried to see himself there, asleep beside her, on the bed of sand.

Three hours. The car crunches on to the track. I am near the town of Hill End. The dust churns behind me, the wheels bouncing over ripples, sliding, like fingers scraped over piano keys. In the twists and turns I am looking for the river.

He surfaced, and felt cheated of his dream. He rubbed the water from his eyes. There were three men on the bank. They stared at him for a long time. Then they began to hurl rocks at him, huge smooth rocks that thudded into the water around him. He dived again, searching for the current, found it, cruised with it.

The sun beats down on my head. Below the rise I can hear the water. It roars when the wind comes rushing up. It makes me nervous as I go down to the river along little narrow sheep tracks. Here and there I can just make out their droppings, pellets scattered like confetti; and all of it speaks of the country, the wind, water, trees, droppings. It all belongs to me.

He rounded another bend, swam towards a sandy bank and, dripping, his clothes heavy, swathes of water still binding him, he emerged and clambered towards the hill before him, tripping over tussocks of dry, bristling grass, clawing at rocks, his heart pounding in his ear. He thought of her, lying sick and hot in the tent. He began to run. He felt the heavy pouch tied to his waist slap at his thigh.

I go down by the water, sit on the uncomfortably smooth rocks. My head aches from the sun. I am panting like a dog. A pain shoots down my left arm. A nerve is drawn tight, hooked to a line in my fingers. There is a heavy rock pinning my chest down. I sweat from the exertion. Yet it was not a long way to come down. The sweat runs into my eyes. The glare intensifies. Water and sun. I discard my clothes. Immediately I am cold, but the wind that dries my skin also loosens the invisible line tugging at the hook attached to the nerve. Soon, too, the rock is lifted from my chest. I float to the surface. I am naked for all to see.

He saw the tent below him. Scrambling down, sending showers of pebbles on to its walls, he reached it. She was lying there, her face puffy, in a sweat, her eyes closed. He wiped her face. She opened her eyes and closed them immediately. He had forgotten to bring the water. A simple task like that had eluded him. He untied the pouch from around his waist and put it on the ground next to her. He would have to get help for her soon. He decided against looking in the pouch. He picked up the water bag and made his way down to the river again. Just below the hill there was an abandoned mine. The opening of the shaft gaped at him from amongst rocks and weeds. He stared into it. Out of habit he had stored most of his provisions and tools just inside the opening. If they raided his tent they would not find anything. He went to the river, filled the bag with clear, unsullied water.

I have brought no provisions. In the end I even decided against the tent and sleeping-bag. The car is up there, though I doubt if I will make it to the top again. I have brought nothing. I wanted myself to feel exactly how he felt in his disillusionment. I wanted to understand my whole history. Will I have the strength to destroy the defences of my own body? I shall lie here and not move. I shall listen to my own breathing, and as long as that is there I will know that I am still alive.

Just as he had feared. When he mopped her brow with the rag dipped in water, he accidentally kicked over the pouch. Shiny pink and blue pebbles fell out. There was nothing that looked like gold. He sat on the ground in a trance. She moaned and called out to him.

Early evening. A strong wind is blowing; perhaps it will rain. Clouds are turning the sky into night faster than the setting sun. There is a strangeness about the cold. A stench passes over me from the opening of a mine shaft just above me. I saw the shaft when I came down. Something has died in there. The beast History feeds there.

He crawled out of the tent before dawn. He could not sleep. The heat was stifling. Mosquitoes buzzed around his ears, stung his face and arms. He scratched himself, feeling the bumps, experienced pain beneath the itch. Suddenly he had an impulse to wade in the river, to cool himself. He scrambled down the slope. He stopped at the mine shaft, squatted, felt around inside. He found the bag, hoisted it out, felt for the paraffin lamp. His fingers closed around something else. A familiar handle nestled in his palm. It was the meat cleaver he had used to slaughter chickens back in his village. He pulled it out. He had not had much use for it. He felt the broad heavy blade. There was a roughness along the edge, and the powdery rust came off on his fingers. He went down to the river with it in his hand.

I was awakened by two men moving slowly past me. They were crouching, stopping, squatting, making a zigzag path to the river. They had not noticed me there, lying naked by the trunks of fallen she-oaks. I tried to get up. It was impossible. I was totally incapable of action.

They jumped on him then, and wrestled him into the water, There was no shouting; hardly a sound. They held him under the water for a long time, the bearded Clancy with a gap between his two front teeth and Carlos, a Spaniard who looked like a bull, with arms the size of hams. Shan struck out with the meat cleaver. There was a hiss of air. He struck blindly, wildly. He felt the cleaver sink into flesh and bone. The grips on him relaxed. A heavy weight fell on top of him. He could not breathe for a long while. He wanted to vomit. A hand covered his face, two of its fingers reaching into his mouth. He bit hard and chopped again. The water swirled into his nostrils. There was a fishy taste of blood. The Spaniard's head loomed up like a balloon hoisted on a pole. Shan chopped at it, sinking the cleaver across the bridge of the nose. With a jerk, the head fell back, taking the cleaver with it, pulling it from his hand. Finally he was able to stand. His lungs whistled as they found air again. He staggered to the bank. One of the men had disappeared into the river. The other lay still in the shallows. Shan panted, squatted beside it. After a few minutes he picked up a leg. He began dragging the body up the slope. It was heavy. He fell, pulled again at the corpse which bumped and thudded over the rocks like a bag of wet sand.

I heard hoofbeats farther up the hill. There was a light. Or was it the first glimmer of sunlight illuminating the top of the hill? Or was it a fire?

He reached the mine shaft, his breath like that of a wild beast. He tipped the body in. Warm blood flowed down his bare arms. It was a long time before he heard the thud. Then a crackling caught his attention. He saw flames, shooting up with sparks and embers from their tips. He ran towards the burning tent, dashed into the flames, dragged at the camp bed, his arms seared. It was empty. He stamped and beat at the flames, kicking down the poles, dragging the charred pieces of canvas away. Mary had disappeared. He sat down on a log.

I was down there. I saw bits of burning paper and large pieces of black ash wafting down the hill over me. The sun burnt through my eyelids and the hexagonal cells filled with blood.

Ching chong Chinaman sitting on a log. Pieces of unburnt yellow paper bowled along in the wind. Husks of his imagination. The breath of something great was denied him. No record, no glimpse of the universal kingdom. He felt the beast in him had surfaced. There was a desperate silence.

He got up, walked slowly towards me with the stealth of a wild animal. He saw a blind man lying naked in the sun. There was a moment of recognition. They seemed to be staring at each other. The blind man thought he had heard a movement, the breath of something alive, quite near. He could feel its warmth.

'Are you really my ancestor, bearing the mark of Cain, standing there with your pigtail pulled off, your face gaunt and haunting?'

The blind man reached for the only article of clothing left to him. It was strange moment to be modest. With the penis gourd in his hand, he struggled pathetically to maintain the last small vestiges of human civilisation.

'Shan!' he shouted.

The visitant bolted into the bush. He had seen his reader: a wriggling, blind, white-haired man spawned by the future on a river bank.

Seamus lay there for a long time. He felt the sun on his eye-lids. Twice he thought he heard the stiff, carpet-beating sound of ducks whirring up the river. He did not expect to notice the passing of time; but there they were, distinct and hard, round-ed moments. The earth shook with them. A branch cracked. Leaves seemed to be spinning down. They sounded like drops of rain when they hit the ground. Between the sounds there was a silence that was total, real. Perhaps this was the prelude to the end. There was no longer even a voice in his head. He felt a release, a purity, a peace.

The compression in his head disappeared. There was a lightness where the cool air entered, flowing down from the mountain of his will, looming up behind him, snow-covered, the current ushering him along, light as a leaf, spinning, float-ing, scraping against the rocks, the wind making a sound like bursts of laughter—or was it sobbing, or both—as footsteps scuffed the sand and arms, soft arms enveloped him, lifted him who was now light as a leaf, cradling him in perfume and warm breath.

Anna Bernhard looked almost ridiculous as she stumbled along, puffing heavily, her burden at her breast, her tears falling like warm rain on his face. She knew she would find him there, knew the place like the back of her hand; knew it when she passed her fingers over the one or two freckles on that hand and thought of the proprieties. She knew it when she stared at the baskets of uneaten scones, great mounds of undigested creation, useless appendages to her emotions. She knew where he was going when she started her car and followed him to the place where she had once lived.

There he was, light as a baby, his open mouth tickling her nipple through the dress. She was sobbing and laughing as though she had found gold, her emotions jumbled, their sources confused. She felt a defiance she was unable to voice.

Nestling deep within her, in her fruitful, voiceless environment, he would be nourished and protected.

5 DEPARTURES

The first thing he experienced when he was allowed to leave the hospital was the affection and the company of women. It was not easy, re-learning openness from the sanctuary into which he had driven himself. It was not easy to rid himself of that preoccupation with self, to learn to trust and accept affection. It was not easy without the capacity for offering it as well.

Edna had invited herself to stay with him in Mrs Bernhard's house. Fatima dropped in regularly, saying very little at first, but paying great attention to him and ministering to his needs. She brought him little gifts, paintings of birds and animals. His room looked like a menagerie. He would place his fingers on the bumpy oils, work out their texture and decide for himself the strength of colours. Anna Bernhard wheeled him about her large house, never leaving him alone for a moment, feeding him on fruit and scones, cooking giant roasts, playing Bach and Beethoven for him on the piano. Just in case, she had removed all the mirrors in the house. In their place she hung silk-screens, or leaves pressed behind glass, or some of Fatima's animal pictures. In the bathroom, where he brushed his teeth with his good arm, he would be facing a fox staring out from the thicket, its face sharp and golden.

All the while the spectre of Shan had not left him. Edna knew this when she read to him and saw his face change, the cheeks drawing themselves in, the eyelids lowering, the trembling chin. Sometimes she thought he was about to say something, and she would lean forward, stopping her reading and waiting for the word. But it would never come. There was just a silent blubbering.

Anna had insisted that Edna stay longer in the house. Together they would look after him. She was not sure why she had been so insistent. She did not really care for Edna's ways, her habit of having brandy bottles underneath the bed, of roaming round the garden in shorts, sandshoes and an old-fashioned bikini top: in her own words, 'collecting a good tan'. She half suspected her insistence was for reasons of insurance. For what? Against what? she asked herself.

She did not like the friendliness Edna cultivated with Fatima, when the latter called in on weekends. She did not like their sitting in the garden under the apple-trees talking in loud voices and laughing, smoking cigarettes; did not like the way Fatima bounced up and down with raucous laughter, her right index finger entwined in her long pearl necklace, her sharp eyes so aware of the slightest trends, the most miniscule changes in atmosphere, in fashion, in the currents of life. She almost hated the two of them when she looked at him sitting there in the shade of the courtyard, the spectre of Shan crossing and recrossing his beleaguered brain. She caught herself hating, yet would have liked to throw in her lot with them: though, of course, she was unable to say anything.

Then it happened one summer's day. It had to happen. The doctors had said so. He uttered something: just two syllables. Edna heard him, but neither of them could make out what he had said. It wasn't the sort of baby sound you would have expected. It was a word begun and ended with fine rounded sounds. Perhaps two words.

As the days went by he spoke other words, words that seemed to connect with the very first one he said. Soon they became tuneful, melodic. Edna thought they were sung. Anna put the sounds to music and played the notes on the piano. Fatima heard them one day and decided they had a freshness and clarity that could be represented only visually.

His sentences grew longer. Throughout the large house you could hear them breezing down corridors like dragonflies attached to thin streams of saliva. They grew louder, too, and the dragonflies became birds, emitting lovely flute-like notes.

One day Edna said it was Chinese. Anna nodded. Fatima chortled. They listened more keenly. At least now they had established that it was a language. They invited the local priest to lunch. He was reputed to be a Chinese scholar.

'Why, yes. Of course,' he said. 'Of course it's Chinese. He is reciting the poetry of Su Tung Po, poet-painter, exiled to South China at the end of the eleventh century, during the northern Sung dynasty.'

But the truth is he did not really know.

Edna continued reading to Seamus. Now and again he would interrupt her reading, shouting out words, breathing whole sentences into life. Edna tried to connect his outbursts with relevant passages from her reading. She could not make much sense out of this, because he would burst in during moments of least perceptible significance. Nevertheless, it was a beginning. She noticed, intelligently persevering in this technique, that there was much more said when she stopped reading Trollope and switched to Kafka. There was a decline when she went from Kafka to James, and then when she read from White he babbled like a cockatoo and rocked in his wheelchair from side to side. Thinking that he might do himself an injury, she kept these readings to small doses.

Anna tried this technique with music. She played the contrasting music of different composers, ready to note any change in his manner or anything he said. She kept a tape-recorder for this purpose. But it did not work. He kept silent, and seemed to be morose. She was offended by his lack of response. The more she persevered, the more deeply hurt she was by his silence.

Then Edna had another coup. She found that he enjoyed radio documentaries and plays. His face bloomed like a flower when he listened. At the end of the programme he would lean back in his chair, sigh and utter long sentences which from their tone (Edna was able to distinguish it now) suggested a profound satisfaction.

Anna began to wonder if he were playing a bizarre game. The thing is, she thought, if he went off into a kind of cynical humour, this would cause a regression. She knew his cure depended on beliefs. She did not know how she could help him, and did not dare admit to herself the only way that was left to her.

It happened suddenly one evening as these things tend to do. When he first blurted it out the two women were in the dining-room. He must have said it a couple of times, because they were barely conscious of that sentence when it came out. He was looking at the ceiling when he said it, and Anna caught the last two words. Five minutes passed before he said it again. She got her notebook and wrote it down.

'A Chinaman, when he is ruined, destroys himself.'

Did he mean that suicide was inevitable in order to save face? Anna wondered whether his attempts to destroy himself were linked with his broken marriage. Or was he speaking about another person?

Then for a month he lapsed into silence. In the evenings the raucous birds screeched themselves to sleep. Anna sat with him, thinking that he might die. She heard the insects take up from where the birds had left off. The nights released fragrances of honey and eucalyptus. Shan had fallen asleep beneath a thicket of tea-trees. Near by, an echidna burrowed in the sand.

He might have been heartless in not going after Mary Young. But only a hero of a more romantic, less realistic fiction would have done this. Since he had killed two men indirectly on account of a woman, the Confucian ideal of the Great Man, the man of the highest calibre, had entirely been destroyed. Furthermore, he could not make himself believe that Mary had been taken away by force. He felt she had abandoned him, betrayed him. It was not hate that rushed into his heart: it was a sense of shame, a loss of face. She had dishonoured him.

He was not entirely wrong to feel this. Mary Young was a woman of vast and complicated resources. For nearly a year she had been informed of Clancy's whereabouts by her numerous friends engaged in the network of prostitution. For almost a year she gave herself to her Chinaman, feeling at the same time the stranglehold of Clancy's jealousy, the strange and methodical way he pursued her with his love. In time she became flattered, then utterly obsessed by his devoted search for her. She learnt of his inquiries through her friends, heard tales of his repentance and regret, was seized by imaginary sagas of his passion, heard he couldn't live without her, how he would rather be dead. Gradually, her attachment to Shan was eroded. She had not been trained by experience to search for the reasons behind emotions that could strengthen their bonds.

It was not out of character, then, for her to have told a friend here and there about her lingering feelings for Clancy. For him, upon hearing this, such feelings amounted to messages of reciprocation and cries for help.

He awoke and remembered a dream. He had seen his reader lying there on the rocks, and had experienced a moment of panic. The feeling was still there. It was a vision of the future; of what he thought was an old man, naked in the womb. It wasn't fanciful. It was a primitive, savage and desperately guilt-ridden vision of his illegitimate progeny. The sense of panic was prolonged. Slowly the full meaning of it dawned on him. He would have to take on alone the responsibility for his lineage, shoulder the burden of being its author. It was a matter of record.

He realized he would now be hunted, not in general terms as part of a race of people, but as an individual. Ruined in the first instance because he believed Mary Young had betrayed him, he would have destroyed himself in depravity and destitution. Hunted as an individual, he made every resolution to survive.

Despite the protests of her friends, despite the suggestions and persuasions of Fatima, who had travelled up from Kiandra in a stagecoach, Mary was determined to raise the child herself. She had already given it her name, having made her decision that night when a wild and drunken German carried her from her tent and placed her in a cart for the long and terrifying ride in to Bathurst. The man had said that Clancy had come for her. He did not say that Clancy was down at the river, trying to kill her Chinaman.

She looked at the baby, its black unseeing eyes moving beneath transparent lids, its fingers curling and uncurling around her nipple.

In another part of the state a town had also been named: Lambing Flat in the Burrangong became known as Young.

Shan kept away from the treachery of roads and tracks. A thick crust of dried blood caked his head; countless flies formed an extra, seething layer. He followed the river away from the goldfields, keeping to areas of thick scrub.

Entering the bush in that wild area was like parting the curtains at the entrance of a vast labyrinth. He wanted to lose himself completely. The deeper in he went, the more alive the bush became. He was surprised at how sharp his vision was: every rock, every tree glowed with a pure light. He detected minute movements of creatures beneath layers of leaves. He saw trees move their branches unaided by the wind. The rocks themselves swelled with hidden life, as if each contained a fire within.

For several weeks he ate goannas and frogs, clubbing them to death while they stared at him with unblinking eyes. When he chewed the rubbery flesh he thought he was dining on platefuls of chicken.

Each morning he marked his course with the sunrise. He thought he had been wandering in precise circles. He came across the bones of a rabbit he thought he had eaten days before, lying there bleached on a rock. Was it another predator that had left the bones there? Even in his lack of direction, which was meant to elude others, there was a guiding principle that he had unconsciously followed; and the principle had led him back to himself. He imagined seeing another survivor in the bush, another who was also himself, camping where he had camped, eating what he had eaten.

He began to head east. Something told him that the ocean was there. He walked by night when he had to cross open country, staying well clear of farms and cottages. By day he slept in the warm sun and observed his surroundings.

One night, as he was drinking from a creek, he heard a noise in the brush. The sounds were not those of animals.

How would one describe Shan's emotions as he peered through the thick scrub at the sight on the road? With his brush and paper he would have been able to paint an exact picture in words of the joy he felt upon seeing the steady human stream moving like a snake in the silence and the night; short, squat men in large straw hats carrying bundles tied to the ends of long poles.

It would be even more different to describe how the stream absorbed him, drew him into it and carried him along; how it ensured his safety within it, clothed him, fed him, and brought him back the way he had come, retracing his own steps, returning, concluding.

The facts, dust-laden and threadbare as they are, we have gleaned from the crumbling molecules of men's memories. They say that Shan returned to Ballarat (there were some rumours that when they found him he had lived for some time with a decimated and forlorn tribe of Aborigines); that at Ballarat he found an uncle who was a wealthy man; that a passage was arranged for him aboard a clipper leaving from Port Melbourne bound for China; that his uncle had given him a sum of money to take back to a waiting wife in Kwangtung province; and that a man by the name of Wang accompanied him to the port to ensure he got on board safely, as well as to take delivery of a consignment of goods.

The facts also tell us that the passage was clean and fast, but not fast enough for Shan. Preparing to resume the life he had led in China, he was also conscious of the immense changes in himself. He was on a different path now, in control of his destiny, and he brought with him something of the void he had experienced in Australia, the silence and the stillness that helped him to accept his microscopic role in the eternal recurrences of nature. Pursued by ghosts threatening to overwhelm him, he willed the ship to fly, its sails shaped into wings by the wind.

Anna Bernhard was listening to the wind. It was so strong that birds flattened themselves on the ground, their neck feathers tufted. They looked like little clods of earth. Despite the howling of the wind she felt a tangible silence, emitted by the man in the wheelchair opposite her.

She was afraid. For months she had wavered between pity and love for him. Now there was a third dimension: fear. She was afraid she would lose him, afraid that having been drawn half-way up the well he was now ready to fall back down for ever.

Having been able to express her pity and love for him only through action, she had no means of showing her fear. She could not speak; her great capacity for feeling could not be expressed in words. Yet she was determined to overcome all distance; and to do this she would have to dive down into that morass of silence, unite her experience with his, and surface on the other side of love. This was the only way left for her.

She walked across to the open door, peered outside. There was a soft clink of glass from Edna's room. She was having her afternoon brandy. Soon sleep would overtake her. Anna breathed in, willed sleep upon her, and locked the door. She walked towards the man.

Slowly, almost too deliberately, she undressed, undoing her blouse which was buttoned up to her throat, stepping out of her skirt, kicking it away from her, reaching behind her back to unhook the brassiere. Naked, except for a pair of velvet and lace panties, she knelt before him, grasping his legs.

His eyes seemed to travel from the nape of her neck along the ridge of dark hair, across her back to her velvet shape. Very slowly he placed a hand on the back of her head. She took his other hand, placed it gently on her breast. Slowly, very slowly, he passed his thumb over the erect nipple. She began to undo his trousers. He seemed to be helping her. Together they wove their motions like butterflies describing the pattern of flowers; hesitant, exploratory.

Outside the wind screamed like a banshee. The birds hunched down low into the grass. He placed a hand on her and felt the softness of fox-fur.

Anna sighed, closed her eyes. She trembled from the touch of his fingers. He was creating her, kneading her. Her mind retreated to a blank world. In it she constructed passion. It was larger than herself. She was in it, this rising wave, gliding off mountains. She was aloft.

'Oh, my God!' she said.

And when she spoke there was a smile on Seamus O'Young's face. He imagined her pretending to the innocence of a child in his hand, while he struggled to swim away; but he tired quickly and the wheelchair was pitching and rolling, and he was in the river watching the current take her and then it took him with her, uniting him with the human stream of which he had never been a part. In one last effort to free himself from it he saw Shan disappearing over the waves towards China, waving like a clownish Ahab aboard the whale.

Released from that other self, he was blubbering and crying and laughing. 'Edna, Edna!' he shouted, in his enlightenment, reaching for the surface. But Edna could not hear him in her sleep. Her role in his past was over.

'Yes, yes!' Anna said, confused, tears of joy in her eyes, her voice sounding new and strange, pure, unknown.

6 THE OTHER LIFE

Kwangtung 1863

I sip the weak tea which has gone cold. My stomach does not want it, and curls up with displeasure. It is raining now, the first time in six years, so they say in the village. I can hear the metallic drops pitting the flimsy roof and already the water finds the hole above my bed. Soon the other leaks will begin and the water will do its best to erase the writing from these sheets. It will show the futility of my life.

My little stove has given up its weak flame. Outside my window, in the blackness, the mountain has disappeared. As I write it seems as though I have just woken from a dream. Funny how writing is not a record for posterity or anything as fanciful, but is really a statement that one is not dreaming. It establishes oneself, puts oneself in control again. It is, I suppose, the discipline of existence.

The rain and the wind gusts beat at the window. In the flashes of distant lightning Australia seems illuminated, thousands of miles away, like a golden myth, harsh in its reality, gentle in its tranquil isolation, and I see my descendant discovering transient moments of joy and laughter, executing portraits in his little book of a time and a place with which I am already too familiar. I feel the presence of the future, hear a voice cutting across mine.

I did not know that when I returned to my village I was returning to death. It was with trepidation that I walked up the road to something which did not remotely resemble a village, but which was a burnt-out shell, the people like ghosts, thin, dirt-covered beings, sick and weak from years of war and famine. Then I saw my father's house, ransacked, destroyed, barely withstanding the wind which rounded the newly terraced hills and raced down to slap at swinging doors, to tear at shreds of ribbon still hanging from dark lintels, my father's prayers for a prodigal son.

It was there that I encountered the old monk who told me of his death, describing to me the quiet, intoxicated sleep-death into which my father had eased himself, relinquishing life as softly as petals falling from the jasmine flower. It was there, too, that the monk had made the offer of his hermitage to me, a shack nestling below the mountain and looking up at the temple that jutted out from the rock, the temple housing the indifferent smile of the Buddha. Having seen many things, my eyes had yet to be opened. I thanked the monk, who was eager to resume what was obviously his last journey.

And I think now that I have found the significance for which I was searching: not in the audacity of mere words, not in the belief in existences that transcend the human, but in the celebration of not searching, in the wonder of the imagination.

Tomorrow, if my strength allows, I shall walk to the town with messages of hope and money for Ah Fung's wife, and I shall tell her that I, too, am waiting, and that a child waits for me.

Brian Castro is the author of *Double-Wolf*, winner of the *Age* Fiction Award and the Victorian Premier's Literary Award. He is also the author of *Pomeroy* and *After China*.

Brilliant, lively, witty, astonishingly assured, strenuously intelligent; these words of praise and many more have been lavished on his work, which can also be admired more simply: for the storytelling which amply rewards the reader.

Brian Castro lives in the Blue Mountains, NSW, where he is currently working on a new novel and a screenplay.

COPYRIGHT

This print edition published in collaboration with Brio Books, an imprint of Booktopia Group Ltd

Level 6, 1A Homebush Bay Drive · Rhodes NSW 2138 · Australia

Print ISBN: 9781761280764

briobooks.com.au

MIX
Paper from responsible sources
FSC® C008194

The paper in this book is FSC® certified. FSC® promotes environmentally responsible, socially beneficial and economically viable management of the world's forests.